DEATH BY GUNPOWDER

Bailiff Mountsorrel Mysteries
Book Six

David Field

SAPERE
BOOKS

Also in Bailiff Mountsorrel Series

The Castle Abductions
The Assassination Players
The Slaughtered Widow
The Clamorous Dead
To Kill A King

DEATH BY GUNPOWDER

Published by Sapere Books.

24 Trafalgar Road, Ilkley, LS29 8HH,
United Kingdom

saperebooks.com

ISBN: 978-0-85495-579-4

Nottingham, England, 1605

Edward Mountsorrel arrived just as the roof timbers of the house in the middle of the inferno — number 6 — began to sag. They fell with a deafening crash, and a shower of sparks forced him to jump backwards sharply to avoid being burned.

The lathe and plaster walls that joined number 6 to the houses on either side of it in the cramped row on Halifax Lane were lines of flame that licked hungrily upwards. The buckets of water being passed from hand to hand were an inadequate response. The only hope lay in the long hooks that were being deployed by the constables under Edward's command, tearing down the outer walls of numbers 5 and 7 in a desperate bid to prevent numbers 4 and 8 from catching fire.

Fire in a row of thatch-roofed houses was the ultimate hazard in the narrow byways of an old town like Nottingham. By 1605 the town authorities had insisted on all new roofs being tiled, but there remained many thatched ones, particularly in poor streets such as this one. Given that the nearest available water was half a mile to the south, in the River Leen, it was likely that once a fierce conflagration like this one took hold, those pulling the water cart would be fighting a losing battle in their attempts to force their way through the thoroughfares crowded with terrified or morbidly curious onlookers.

'Why did you get me out of bed in the middle of the night?' Edward asked Senior Constable Jack Durward, raising his voice in order to be heard above the screams and pleas for assistance. Durward jerked his head to the right, where what looked like a large bundle of discarded clothing lay in the roadway. Edward nodded and moved across to examine the singed corpses of two men, a woman, and a child of around ten years of age.

Durward had followed him. 'Tom and Agnes Whitely, from number seven, along with their lass Catherine,' he bellowed in Edward's ear. 'Don't know who the other man is, but word has it that he were renting number six, where the fire started. They reckon there were a big bang first of all, then it went up in flames.'

Edward still didn't understand why he'd been required to leave his warm bed on a frosty night in the middle of November. He was the bailiff to the joint Sheriffs of Nottingham, Robert Freeman and Anthony Gamble, and attending fires was not one of his responsibilities. There were enough other occasions when his presence would be required in some dismal part of the old town at a thoroughly unreasonable hour. But then Jack Durward nodded again at the body of the man he'd identified as Thomas Whitely, and Edward took a closer look.

The smoke had blackened his face, and the flames had singed his clothing, but that was not what had killed him. Edward was no physician, but he had learned to recognise the gaping hole left in a tunic by a pistol ball. He had seen many such holes during his time as a foot soldier in the infantry company assembled some years ago by Robert Dudley, the late Earl of Leicester, in anticipation of a landfall by the troops aboard the Spanish Armada. Thomas Whitely had been shot, probably murdered, and this *was* something that required Edward's attention.

'Well spotted, Jack,' said Edward. 'What can you tell me about him?'

'Tom Whitely owned The Pilgrim, sir, down by the castle rock — the alehouse that used to be The Crusader, if you remember.'

Edward certainly remembered that particular hovel, from his days as bailiff to the county sheriff. The granting of a charter to Nottingham just over two centuries ago had separated the town from the county that surrounded it, and given it a sheriffdom of its own, traditionally occupied by two office-bearers. The county had continued to be governed by the office-holder designated as Sheriff of Nottinghamshire, and the ancient medieval castle, on the western boundary of the town, fell under the county's jurisdiction. Likewise the buildings that lay at the bottom of the 130-foot-high natural sandstone escarpment on which the castle had been constructed.

One of those buildings had begun as the brewhouse to the castle, located conveniently on the banks of the River Leen, from which water might be drawn for brewing. At some time in the past the brewhouse had been transformed into a public alehouse, and subsequent generations of dissolute landlords serving a rowdy, depraved clientele had contrived to give it an evil reputation. As county bailiff Edward had been obliged to visit the hovel almost daily. He still had nightmares about the time he'd uncovered a trade in human misery, connived at by a former landlord, Jeb Tanner. Tanner had turned a blind eye to prostitutes being drugged and incarcerated inside the network of caves that led from the ground floor of The Crusader up into the castle rock. The women had been destined for a life of sexual slavery in Scotland until Edward had discovered the trade and put a stop to it. The serving girl who'd supplied him with the tip-off had been murdered by Tanner, who had in due course been hanged.

Oh yes, Edward was familiar with the premises, and he pulled a face when he heard who this dead man, Tom Whitely, had been. But fortunately for Edward it was no longer his business what went on inside The Pilgrim, as it was now called. That particular burden had been transferred to his good friend, former town bailiff Francis Barton. Francis had become the county bailiff some years ago, when the two men had exchanged roles.

However, their long friendship, along with the requirement that the two officials work in tandem when needed, obliged Edward to save Francis unnecessary enquiries when he was able.

'Is The Pilgrim the same filthy, degenerate establishment that it always was?' he asked Jack, who shook his head. The town constables found it convenient to spend their leisure hours drinking in alehouses that did not form part of their territory, so Jack was able to give Edward the necessary background.

'Tom Whitely was doing his best to make the place respectable again,' said the constable. 'There were still prostitutes using the place to pick up marks, but they weren't allowed to do the business in there. And anyone who got really drunk was lobbed out.'

'Let's hope that the next landlord follows Tom's example,' Edward replied grimly, 'if only for the sake of my county colleague. But our immediate task is to find out how Tom came to die. Have the bodies taken down to the usual place under the Guildhall until someone claims them for burial. But you reckon that this second man's a stranger to you?'

Jack looked back down at the smoke-blackened corpse and nodded. 'Like I said, they reckon he was renting number six from Tom Whitely. Seems that Tom owned the whole row. But it looks to me as if the fire started in number six, and I was told that there was a big bang afore the place went up in flames, so how come this man doesn't look so badly burned as Tom?'

Edward looked back at the three houses that were almost certainly due for demolition, given the extent of the damage. 'The middle one's certainly the worst affected, which suggests that it was where the fire started. But could the bang you were told about have been the sound of a pistol being discharged?'

Jack shrugged. 'Could have been, I suppose, but from the way it was described to me, I think it was louder than that. Then again, how many folks around here have ever heard a pistol shot?'

'None, if we've been doing our job properly,' said Edward. 'But once the bodies have been removed, I want a very thorough search of all three houses to be conducted. For one thing, there could be a pistol lying around somewhere in there, and I don't want it to fall into the wrong hands. So tell the men to search *very* carefully once the embers have cooled sufficiently to allow them in.'

'I will, sir.'

Edward decided to call it a night. He'd travelled on foot from his home in Whitefriars Lane when called out by the urgent hammering on his front door by Jack Durward, so he walked swiftly through the twisted tangle of the old lanes that lay between his house and Halifax Lane, hoping to lose the smell of smoke from his clothing. When he arrived, he lifted the latch to the front door as quietly as the rusting metal permitted, pulled off his cloak and threw it to its usual place nearby. He heard a hiss of disapproval and peered into the gloom.

'I don't know why you bothered to nail up that hook near the door,' his wife Elizabeth complained in a whisper, 'since I've never once seen you use it.'

'You're awake early,' Edward said unnecessarily.

'We *all* are, thanks to whoever attacked our front door in the middle of the night. And what was all that shouting about, down in the town?'

'There was a fire in Halifax Lane.'

'So why did they need you?'

'Jack Durward spotted that one of the victims had been murdered.'

'The fire was deliberately set, you mean?'

'It's not as straightforward as that, I'm afraid,' Edward replied. He moved further into the room to find his three eldest children sitting at the table. 'Is there any breakfast yet?'

'Not yet.'

'And we are hungry,' eight-year-old Joanna complained, while her older brother Robert just stared sullenly at the table. The eldest child, twelve-year-old Margaret, looked back down at the tapestry she was working on by the flickering light of a candle.

'I'll be through in a minute, Mistress,' their house servant Meg promised as she peered round the scullery door. 'I didn't sleep any better than the household, so I'll put a pot on to boil and see what's left in the larder. A bit of salted pork, likely, but the bread's two days old now. I'll get more at the market.'

'It'll be light soon,' Edward said as he peered through the open scullery door and out into the garden that lay beyond it, where the kitchen was located, with Meg's modest accommodation to one side of it.

'Then I suppose you'll be back out there again, searching for a murderer?' Elizabeth asked. She'd always objected to Edward's almost continual absence as he went about his duties with a commendable enthusiasm that was somehow never appreciated by any of his employers. By the time the town sheriffs were replaced every March, they'd just begun to realise how fortunate they were to have a man of Edward's calibre as their bailiff. But then the office was transferred to the next two in line, and Edward was required to earn his spurs anew. It was the same for Francis in the county, but he had only one sheriff to deal with each year, whereas Edward had two. Like the current two, they frequently fell out, making Edward's life even more difficult.

'I can hardly ignore a murder,' Edward replied, 'but it may be that this one will fall to Francis.'

'It happened in the town, surely?' Elizabeth asked.

'It did, but the victim was Tom Whitely, landlord of The Pilgrim.'

'That dreadful place under the castle?'

'The very same, although according to Jack Durward it's become more respectable lately, ever since it stopped being The Crusader. Tom Whitely took it over and changed its name in order to improve its reputation.'

'It could hardly have got any worse,' Elizabeth replied with a grimace.

'Is Uncle Francis going to be visiting us, if there's work for him down here?' Margaret asked eagerly. Francis was her favourite person, and had been for as long as she could remember. She got on well with his wife Kitty as well, and was forever bossing around their eldest child, Richard, now seven years old.

'Whether or not he'll need to come down here remains to be seen,' Edward replied. 'But he won't know he has a choice unless I go up to Daybrook and tell him. So,' he added as he inclined his head towards Elizabeth, 'I won't be home for dinner.'

'Now, *there's* a change,' Elizabeth replied with heavy sarcasm. 'The only way I'm ever likely to see you at dinner in this house is if I murder someone. Or set fire to the place, seemingly.'

2

'You're more than a month too late for the apple harvest,' Francis said as he watched Edward dismounting outside the house set back from the orchard that he owned with his wife Kitty. They had two children — Richard and little Amy, who stood sucking her thumb while standing shakily upright in the doorway, with her other hand wrapped in the hand of her Aunt Rose, Kitty's sister, who also resided with the family.

'I came for the cider, not the raw ingredients,' Edward replied, 'and by an unhappy coincidence I'm also here to report a murder.'

Five minutes later, they were sitting around the table in the kitchen, and Kitty set down a platter of fresh bread and homemade cream cheese.

'Since when did the town bailiff report murders to the county bailiff?' she asked suspiciously.

'We may be obliged to work together on this one,' Edward explained. 'While the murder took place in the town, the victim was running an alehouse on its western extremities, just inside the county.'

'Not that bloody place under the castle rock again?' Francis complained. 'The behaviour in there may have improved, but the ale tastes as if it was strained through the landlord's hose.'

'Perhaps that's why he was murdered,' said Edward.

Francis raised his eyebrows. 'So it *was* that Tom Whatshisname, was it?'

'Tom Whitely, that's right. But it's not straightforward, I'm afraid. We found his body following a house fire. It was lying outside a row of three old houses in Halifax Lane, but the fire itself seems to have broken out first in the house next door, then spread to his house.'

'Then what makes you think he was murdered?'

'Something to do with the pistol ball in his chest,' Edward replied wryly. 'His wife and daughter were also seemingly killed in the same fire, along with an unidentified man who was renting the house next door. That man wasn't as badly burned as the others, and may even have choked to death on the smoke.'

'I've known a few die that way,' Rose Middleham chimed in. Kitty's older sister was a 'wise-woman' who Edward had rescued several years ago, when she'd been in danger of being hanged as a witch. In the process, he'd unwittingly become the matchmaker between Kitty and Francis.

'Can we not talk about something else?' Kitty complained. 'The only time we ever get to see Edward is when he's getting Francis involved in some investigation or other, and by the sound of things this occasion is no different. So how are Elizabeth and the children?'

'Do I detect that Kitty resents your calling as much as Elizabeth does mine?' Edward asked Francis, who gave a pained nod as Edward continued, 'Elizabeth is in fine health, I'm delighted to report, although her temper does not improve with age. She's approaching forty years old, and somehow that's all my fault.'

Rose gave a loud chuckle. 'She's experiencing that difficult time when women's bodies rebel against all that men have put them through. I can give you a simple for that, but I can't change your employment, and it's that which she's really taking issue with, is it not? She's all alone in the house, with four children to deal with. And the oldest — the girl with those beautiful blue eyes — she must be reaching a time of great bodily change as well.'

Edward nodded. 'Margaret's going to be thirteen on her next birthday, and some girls her age are already being hawked on the marriage market by the nobility. Fortunately for us, she's already decided on her life partner — she's determined to marry Francis.'

'There are days when she'd be welcome to him,' Kitty said ruefully, 'but as long as he can still heft apple barrels, I'll keep him, thank you very much.'

'What about Robert?' Rose asked. 'I seem to recall that as a small child he was somewhat withdrawn.'

'He still is, in many ways,' Edward replied, 'but I shall always be grateful to you for giving me that simple to help him. It brought him out from what seemed like a black hole into which his mind had sunk.'

'In return for which, you saved me from a hanging,' Rose reminded him, 'so that account was squared long since. How are the other two?'

'Joanna's eight now, and eating us out of house and home,' Edward replied. 'As for Edwin, the youngest, imagine a two-year-old who can sleep as easily as the elderly man he's named after — Elizabeth's father, back in Ashby.'

'I remember when he was born there, two days after our little Amy,' said Kitty as she hugged the silent, curly-haired little girl to her side. 'You were both absent, of course, smoking out traitors down south.'

'Talking of smoke,' said Francis, 'there was a reason why Edward took the trouble to ride for two hours up here, other than to sample our board and dispense intelligence regarding his family. And if he misses supper at home as well as dinner, Elizabeth will be marking me out for her barbed tongue, as well as him. He presumably requires my assistance with the investigation into the murder of Tom Whitely.'

'I will certainly require your authority, if not your actual assistance, in learning more about Tom Whitely,' Edward confirmed. 'He was reasonably wealthy, I assume, so could the motive for his death have been robbery?'

'Possibly,' Francis conceded, 'but Tom was also wise, and very careful with his money. I'd hazard a guess that he had most of his wealth spirited away in the vaults of some local merchant with the necessary facilities. And there'd be a great deal to store away, I believe. Apart from owning and managing The Pilgrim, he had quite a few properties in the town that he rented out to others. The whole of that row in Halifax Place, for example, so the stranger who you haven't yet identified was almost certainly his tenant. Perhaps it was a disagreement regarding unpaid rent that led to his death.'

'Perhaps,' said Edward, 'but I'm anxious to know if he had either friends or tenants who were unsavoury enough to own a pistol, or if he owned one of his own.'

'He could have been forgiven for that, if he had,' said Francis, 'considering the amount of coin that he'd need to take from his alehouse to his home, or to his merchant with the underground vault, on an almost daily basis.'

'Do you know if he had any enemies?' Edward asked hopefully.

'Name any clergyman in the town. Tom had succeeded in preventing prostitutes from actually doing their business on his premises, but old habits die hard, and the women still tried to hang around his taproom until he spotted them and had them thrown out. But they were still welcome if they came in with a man on their arm, and the wiser ones were in the habit of hanging around in the lane, inviting men to accompany them inside. The local parsons tried to get the place closed down more than once. Then there were the drunks who were regularly thrown out of there by his fixers, and told not to come back. They must have sorely resented being frozen out of their favourite watering hole.'

'Will you take offence if I go in there and make enquiries into the names of such people — prostitutes and drunks who may have borne Tom a grudge?' Edward asked.

Francis shook his head. 'I'll only take offence if you do so without me. Apart from safety in numbers — for The Pilgrim is still not exactly Canterbury Cathedral — you'll need an escort when you begin to question the prostitutes in there, so that Elizabeth can't accuse you of combining duty with pleasure.'

'Perhaps you'd care to stay with us when you come down to join me?' Edward suggested.

'Perhaps he *wouldn't*!' Kitty protested. 'Either he comes home after completing his investigations, or he can find another apple orchard in which to lay his head!'

An hour later, Francis accompanied Edward to the stables.

'Sorry for getting you into trouble with Kitty,' Edward muttered sheepishly as he walked his latest horse, Oliver, from the stable and swung into the saddle.

'Not your fault,' Francis assured him. 'It comes with the job, as you have learned. Let's just find a swift answer to your questions, shall we?'

The following morning, Edward was seated behind his desk in his room below the Guildhall when he looked up to see a smiling Jack Durward in his doorway. He was carrying a calico sack, from which he began extracting various items and placing them on Edward's desk.

'This is what we got from the houses in Halifax Lane,' he explained. 'Well, to be honest with you, they all come from number six. There was other stuff, but these looked the most interesting, as you can see.'

'Number six was the house in the middle, where the fire probably started?' Edward checked, and as Durward nodded, Edward picked up the pistol. 'This probably explains how Tom Whitely got shot,' he observed, 'which then raises two more questions — why, and by whom?'

'The man who was living there?' Durward suggested.

'A reasonable first assumption, but these may tell more of the story.' Edward was handling one of three hoops of slightly rusted metal, each of which appeared to have been broken with considerable force. He weighed them in his hand for a moment, then asked, 'What do these look like to you?'

'Metal hoops, like you get on barrels?' Durward suggested.

'And what's stored in barrels?'

'Ale, obviously, and grain. Sometimes fruit, like apples and pears.'

Edward chuckled. 'It's easy to see that you have no military experience. They use barrels to store gunpowder.'

Durward's face lit up as something occurred to him. 'That'd explain the big bang that some folks reckon they heard just before the place went up in flames!'

'It also explains what led to the fire,' said Edward. 'And I'll take a wild guess that what caused the gunpowder to go off was some sort of flash from the pistol.'

'Not the shot itself?'

'No, more likely carelessness in using the weapon while firing,' Edward told him. 'A pistol works by applying a length of lit fuse to what they call the flash pan. This is filled with gunpowder, and when it ignites it sets off the powder in the touch hole in the barrel, and it's this that sends the ball on its way to the target. I can see by your face that this is all new to you, but when I was an infantryman I spent hours learning how to use it without killing myself, or those around me. The most dangerous thing was the fuse itself, which had to be kept lit all the time for quick application to the flash pan. There was a risk of burning your own hand, or setting off the flash pan by accident, or holding the barrel too close to your face when the flash came. For obvious reasons, we also kept a supply of gunpowder in a powder horn, and if that caught light you could be seriously burned, or even killed.'

'And you reckon that's what happened when that man shot at Tom Whitely?'

'Something worse than that,' said Edward. 'If there was loose gunpowder lying around in number six, or even a barrel that had been opened, and somehow either the fuse fell into it, or a spark from it blew into the powder, that would explain the big bang, followed by the fire.'

'So we know how it maybe happened, then?'

'Yes, we do,' said Edward, frowning, 'but what we have yet to learn is *why* it happened, and who the mysterious tenant of number six might have been. Have you got the men making further enquiries into that?'

'I certainly have,' Durward confirmed, 'but so far nobody seems to know anything about him other than that he only came and went when it was dark. Otherwise, he kept himself to himself, even nailing up the shutters over the windows.'

'Well, keep going with that,' Edward instructed him. 'In the meantime, when Bailiff Barton arrives from the county, show him down here immediately, if he doesn't just stride past the door guard as if he owns the place. There was a time when he did my job, so he knows where everything is.'

Edward was just starting to conclude that Kitty had persuaded her husband that his journey wasn't really necessary when his doorway darkened again, and there stood Francis, holding a handful of coins.

'I predict that a certain pie seller in Weekday Cross is about to do some business,' he announced. 'I could eat a horse, which is perhaps as well, because some days I believe that's what the mountebank puts in his pies.'

3

Since the Guildhall was the principal building in Weekday Cross, Edward and Francis only had to walk a few paces to purchase two meat pies from the stall at the side of the roadway. They then sat down on the Guildhall steps, turning their faces up to the pale sky while they allowed their pies to cool a little.

'Make the best of the fresh air while you can,' Francis warned Edward, 'because it will be in short supply once we enter The Pilgrim.'

'I *have* been there before,' Edward reminded him, 'although in those days it was called The Crusader, and it was dangerous for anyone like ourselves, representing the law, to go in there without an escort of armed soldiers. You may also recall that nasty little doorway that led from the end of the back corridor up into the castle dungeons.'

'I certainly remember the dungeons,' Francis said with a grimace, 'because my skeleton would still be mouldering away in one of them if you hadn't rescued me. Consider these meat pies your reward.'

'You've repaid that debt many times over,' Edward replied, 'particularly when you did for the man who murdered my mother.'

'You have no proof that I did that,' said Francis with mock severity, 'and I don't intend to confess. But should you choose to believe that, then these meat pies are an added precaution against what awaits us in The Pilgrim, assuming that it's still open after Tom Whitely's death.'

'How can meat pies protect us from evil?' Edward asked.

Francis chuckled. 'They'll stop us being tempted to consume anything in The Pilgrim. Now, once you've wiped the grease from your chin, shall we go?'

It was only early afternoon, but The Pilgrim appeared to be well patronised already, to judge by the noise that was audible even as Edward and Francis walked along the narrow path that ran along the north bank of the Leen. In the rear doorway lay a man covered in vomit that was hopefully his own, and when they walked through the narrow entrance into the taproom and approached the serving counter, Francis couldn't help himself.

'Just to let you know that your sign's fallen down outside,' he told the burly and seemingly humourless man who was filling pots from a huge container.

'If you mean that smelly drunk that spewed up all over my counter, then we're well rid of him,' the man replied. 'You wanting a pot of this special barley mash that the brewers delivered fresh this morning?'

'You mean that the delivery was fresh, but that the ale isn't necessarily?' Edward quipped.

The man blew out his cheeks as he gave them both a disapproving frown. 'Two jesters in the one delivery — how blessed I feel. I bet the king's missing you both already. D'you want some ale, or would you prefer to leave?'

'Actually,' Edward replied sternly, 'we'd like to ask you some questions. I'm Bailiff Mountsorrel from the town, and this is Bailiff Barton from the county. It's about the death of Thomas Whitely. Given that the landlord of this place is dead, I suppose my first question must be what's your authority to be behind that counter?'

'Tom Whitely was married to my sister, Aggie,' the man replied. 'I'm Will Bestwood, and until we work out who gets what, the family wants me to keep this place going. But why the two of you? Does one of you need a wet nurse, or what?'

'No, we need answers,' Francis persisted. 'As to your very pertinent question, your brother-in-law was murdered in the town, but this alehouse is located in the county.'

'So he *was* murdered, then? We were all wondering about that. Not like him to set fire to one of his own houses, skinflint that he was.'

'Did you know the man who was renting the house next door to his?' Edward asked.

Bestwood spat into the sawdust at his feet. 'No, but I wouldn't be surprised to learn that he murdered Tom. They were doing some business or other, but I reckon it must have gone sour. He was a shifty-looking man who called himself Cuthbert, and he said he'd been sent by Tom's brother to see to something important, though Tom never got round to telling me what it was about.'

'So Tom Whitely had a brother, did he?' Edward asked.

Bestwood undid the apron from around his waist and called to a sallow-looking man by his side to take over the service of ale. He then moved to the far end of the counter, lifted a flap and walked out into the taproom, gesturing for Edward and Francis to follow him into the rear corridor that Edward remembered so well. They all took a seat in one of the curtained booths that ran down its length.

'Can't be too careful about who might overhear what, these days,' Bestwood muttered, then took up the story without further prompting. 'Tom Whitely and his brother Robert come from money — a big house up near Skegby, or somewhere like that. It's near the Derbyshire border, anyroad, so far as I can recall. Tom was the older brother by a few years, and they were both sent down into Nottingham to attend the grammar school in Stoney Street. Tom never took to all that learning, preferring to follow his father into cattle farming, which is how they'd made their money. But the younger brother, Robert — well, he was different, see, and the schoolmaster that ran the grammar school got him into religion. He was a Catholic priest, you see — the schoolmaster, that is — even though it was against the law to worship like that, even in the old queen's later days. To come to the point, young Robert got himself arrested for preaching the Mass in a big house in Derbyshire somewhere, and the last we heard he was in a prison down in London, and nobody talked about him. Tom was ashamed of him, to tell the truth, but he *was* his brother, after all, and you can't help your feelings, now, can you?'

'And this man — "Cuthbert", was that his name? — he arrived here to tell Tom that he had news of his brother?' Edward asked.

'That's what he said,' Bestwood confirmed. 'Whatever it was, Tom let him stay free of charge in that house next door — the one that caught fire. I never liked the look of the man, to be honest, and it's still against the law to do anything Catholic, isn't it? So maybe there was something suspicious about the whole bloody business. It got poor old Tom killed, anyroad.'

Edward glanced at Francis with a grimace. 'That melody sounds familiar, does it not?'

Francis nodded, then turned back to Bestwood. 'Thank you, Master Bestwood. You've been of considerable assistance to the justice process, whether you wanted to be or not.'

'Before we depart, could you tell us whether there was anyone else living in your sister and brother-in-law's house at the time of the fire?' Edward asked. 'We found three bodies — your sister, your brother-in-law, and a young girl who was presumably your niece.'

'There were a couple of servants, that's all — a maid called Lucy, and a steward who called himself Benjamin. But they were both lazy, and had probably gone for the night when the fire happened.'

'Yes, it sometimes pays to be slothful,' Edward commented as he rose to his feet. 'As we can see all around us. Keep up the good work, Mr Bestwood.'

'Did you really have to insult him just as we were leaving?' Francis protested as they walked back across Greyfriars Meadow. 'He was doing his best to help us.'

'You think so?' Edward replied with raised eyebrows. 'I think he was doing his best to keep something very important from us. No doubt something to do with that plague pit that he has the impertinence to call an alehouse.'

The sun was beginning to slide down behind the castle to the west as they walked back through the front entrance to the Guildhall. When the doorkeeper saw Edward, he shouted eagerly, 'There's some man in your room, sir! I asked him the nature of his business, and he told me to mind my own, and threatened to have me locked in one of our cells if I refused to show him where your room was. He seemed very insistent.'

'We'll soon put him in his place,' Edward assured him grimly. He and Francis all but ran down the stairs to the open door of Edward's room, where a middle-aged man sat in the chair behind Edward's desk, holding a scroll of parchment. Edward was first through the door, and demanded angrily, 'Who the hell are you, and what authority have you to take over my office?'

The man looked up lazily, then unrolled the parchment and handed it to Edward. He paled as he cast his eyes over it, then silently handed it to Francis for him to do likewise. It read:

Know all men by these presents that the bearer of this document is thereby authorised to do all such things, and make all such enquiries, as may be necessary in order to bring to justice all traitors against my throne. Those who resist, molest or otherwise hinder my loyal servant in the performance of his sworn duty shall be adjudged traitors and shall pay the awful penalty therefore.

   By my hand,

   James, by the Grace of God, King of England

4

'You come directly from the king?' Edward asked, wide-eyed.

The man gave a wan smile as he shook his head. 'Not directly, no. My name is Walter Emerson, and my immediate instructions come from the attorney general, Sir Edward Coke. It was he who arranged for me to bear this note from His Majesty that gives me such wide authority. I'm here seeking traitors to the Crown.'

'Then we share similar functions,' Edward replied. 'My colleague and I have been of assistance in such matters in the past. The gentleman standing beside me is Francis Barton, bailiff for Nottinghamshire, and I am Edward Mountsorrel, bailiff for Nottingham. How may we be of assistance *this* time?'

'This may take a little while to explain,' Emerson replied, 'and it might be easier if you were both seated.'

It was the work of a moment for Francis and Edward to carry in the bench from outside, and place it in front of the desk that Emerson had commandeered. Then they sat expectantly, like errant schoolboys summoned by their headmaster, until Emerson opened up regarding his mission.

'You have presumably heard that there was a recent planned attempt on the king's life that was fortunately foiled?'

'We heard that there was a plot to assassinate him when he opened the new session of Parliament,' Edward confirmed. 'It was one of those matters revealed to us by our sheriffs not two weeks ago.'

'Indeed, and in due course your immediate employers will be told that you are now to give priority to the king's business, rather than frittering away your time breaking up alehouse brawls and hauling prostitutes out of alleyways.'

'You have not yet spoken with them?' Francis asked.

Emerson shook his head. 'It is far more important that I lose no time in instructing those on the ground who are in the best position to root out those who are scattered across the nation, hiding from the consequences of their part in the failed plot. I am destined to cover every county of the nation in due course, and this is only my third week on the road.'

'But if the plot was in London...' Francis began, then stopped when Emerson raised his hand for silence.

'The plot was indeed intended to have its first manifestation in London — to be precise, within the Parliament Chamber in the Palace of Westminster. But its many facets involved pockets of treason throughout the realm, and its ultimate goal was a change of monarch.'

'Catholics again?' Edward asked.

'Yes, among others,' Emerson confirmed. 'There are many throughout the land who would welcome someone other than James Stuart on the throne of England, but I will not dwell on that aspect of the matter, since time is short and I must be in Lincoln before nightfall. Let us assume, for the sake of what follows, that the principal players in the intrigue were of a Catholic persuasion.'

'They have plotted against the king at least twice in the past,' Edward reminded him, 'and Francis and I were part of the process that laid bare their plans and brought those responsible to justice.'

'Of this I am well aware,' Emerson replied, 'having spoken with the Earl of Huntingdon during my brief meeting with him earlier today. He speaks highly of your previous exploits, and assures me that I may place absolute trust in you both.'

'You have been in Ashby?' Edward asked. 'My wife's family reside there.'

'This I also know,' said Emerson, 'and I would ask that you adopt your former practice of communicating through the earl when you have matters to report to London. He will know to whom to dispatch the messenger, and of course you may employ, as your cover, the need to visit family.'

'So what do you wish us to do?' Francis asked, his spirits sinking at the prospect of being away from his family.

'I wish you to smoke out those in this county who might have been involved in the murderous plot that would have wiped out half the nobility of England, and replaced them with puppets of Rome. How much have you learned of what was intended by the traitors?'

'Merely that they were intent on killing the king,' Edward admitted.

Emerson shook his head sadly. 'It was much more than that, as I can reveal. But perhaps it might be wise to close that door behind you.'

Edward did as requested, and the atmosphere somehow became more oppressive as Emerson leaned back in his chair, raised his eyes to the ceiling, and recalled the events in question for the benefit of yet another under-informed audience.

'On the fifth of November past, His Majesty was to preside at the State Opening of the new Parliament. This was to take place in the House of Lords, and in accordance with tradition the ceremony would be attended by not only all the members of both houses, but also the additional members of the Privy Council, the senior judges and all the bishops of the Church of England. It was also believed that the queen would be in attendance, and possibly the heir apparent Henry, along with his younger brother Charles. The intention was to kill them all in one monstrous act of evil that would leave the nation effectively ungoverned for as long as it took for the conspirators to form a government of their own. The remaining royal child, nine-year-old Princess Elizabeth, would have been the titular queen, but under the control of a Regency Council consisting of leading Catholics who would immediately contact Rome for papal absolution of their sins, and the appointment of a new Catholic Archbishop of Canterbury.'

Both Edward and Francis sat with their mouths open at the sheer audacity of it, until something occurred to Francis.

'How could they bring about so many deaths at the same time?'

'Gunpowder,' Edward answered without hesitation.

Emerson looked impressed. 'Your days under Leicester were clearly not wasted. So perhaps you'd care to suggest where it might be best to place gunpowder in such a way as to maximise the damage?'

'Clearly, somewhere underneath the building,' Edward suggested.

Emerson nodded. 'Thank God that you are on our side, Mountsorrel — or did you have some involvement in the plot yourself?'

'Absolutely not,' Edward insisted, unsure if Emerson was jesting or not. 'But we are ourselves investigating the dreadful consequences of what may have been an accident with gunpowder here in the town only two days past. I am now wondering whether the two events might be linked. But how would gunpowder from London come to be here in Nottingham so soon after the event that you describe?'

'There was certainly plenty of it,' said Emerson. 'Thirty-six barrels in total, and, as you rightly conjecture, they were planted immediately beneath the House of Lords, with a long fuse already set. Fortunately, the gunpowder was discovered on the night before the fuse was due to be lit, and the man caught with it — a rogue calling himself "Johnson" — is currently entertaining our most skilled torturers in the Tower of London.'

'But clearly there were others involved?' Edward prompted.

'Clearly. Which is why I am destined to travel the length and breadth of the nation, and you must search every inch of the town and county, looking for those who must have formed part of the broader conspiracy. We have so far learned from the man Johnson — whose real name is apparently "Fawkes" — that the explosion in Parliament was to be the signal for the seizure of all the royal castles and other palaces of strategic importance. York, for example, in order to secure the north; this was where the plotters intended to house the new Queen Elizabeth, safe from any prospect of rescue. They also intended to seize Chester, Warwick, Lincoln and Nottingham. This city's castle guards one of the few crossings of the Trent, for any army seeking to head to York along the Old North Road.'

'But if the plot was foiled, then presumably any armed rebellion is at an end?' Francis argued.

'For the moment, possibly,' Emerson agreed, 'but if the network of traitors is left unbroken, they could soon re-form and strike again. At present they are scattered around the nation, and my mission is to identify them, arrest them and have them disposed of for good.'

'What exactly happened when this man — "Fawkes", did you call him? — was discovered, and the first part of the plot failed?' Edward asked.

Emerson frowned. 'Obviously, since there was a conspiracy, and we did not know who else might have been involved, we questioned Fawkes very closely and painfully. By the time he began to give us names, those he named had fled, and we have no idea who the remainder may have been, how many of them there were, and where they may be now. Hence my mission.'

'What do you know of those that fled?'

'We closed the city gates almost immediately after the plot was discovered, but we believe that the main conspirators had succeeded in leaving before then,' said Emerson with a sigh. 'Of course, some of them may still be skulking in low places in London — Lord knows there are enough of them. The only name of significance that we got out of Fawkes was that of Robert Catesby — we know him to be an able swordsman who should have been hanged following his part in the failed Essex Rebellion some years ago. Instead he was allowed by the late queen to escape with a large fine, and this is how he repays us.

'Our agents across the water tell us that he was in communication with the Spanish in an attempt to persuade them to invade once the king and all the others were dead, but that the Pope dissuaded King Philip. Catesby then seems to have put together a large group of dissidents with differing talents to contribute to the plot. Some of them had little more to offer than money, but some could also provide safe houses in which to meet and seek sanctuary should ought go amiss, as it obviously did. We know that Catesby led a group that raided Warwick Castle for further supplies — mainly of horses and gunpowder — which were carried off in barrels by wagon, and we have one of the wagon masters in secure custody in the Tower. He assures us that he acted under duress, but that he made a delivery to a place called Holbeche, which is in

Staffordshire. He was then allowed his freedom, but servants at Holbeche, under intense questioning by men under my command, informed us that a sizeable body of men led by Catesby were heard making plans to ride hard to a country house at Boningale, on the Staffordshire border, owned by a relative of one of the conspirators. They were posing as a hunting party, but we currently have both Boningale and Holbeche surrounded by armed men of our own.'

'How do you know that you don't have them all?' Francis asked.

Emerson sighed with irritation. 'Did I not already tell you that we don't know how many of them there are? That being the case, how can we possibly know if we have them all?'

'Clearly, if they were planning on capturing all the castles to which you refer, including ours, there must be an army of them hiding under cover, or simply awaiting their next instruction,' Edward added, hoping to restore their credentials as bailiffs.

'Precisely,' Emerson agreed. 'And it is your appointed task to identify the likely suspects here in Nottingham, then hold them in secure custody until we can transfer them south. When you have done so — and not before — simply advise the Earl of Huntingdon.'

'Can you supply us with any names that we might begin with?' Edward asked.

'The nearest to you geographically is a man named Robert Keyes. He began life promisingly enough, as the son of the Protestant rector of the parish church in a place called Staveley, to the north of Derbyshire.' He paused as he saw the look of interest that flashed across Edward's face. 'You know of the place?'

'It was mentioned in a recent conversation,' Edward confirmed, 'but please continue.'

'Well, somehow or other it seems that Keyes became ensnared by Catholic promises of great reward, both here and in the afterlife. Whatever means they employed, Keyes became a desperate man, ruined and indebted by the reversals he suffered when he refused to recant his beliefs. It would seem that he therefore kept house for Catesby in London, in a hovel of sorts across the river. The gunpowder was stored there prior to its being rowed across to Westminster under cover of night. He'd married a widow called Christina, who was employed as the governess to the children of Baron Mordaunt. We believe Mordaunt was also involved in the plot, and he has his main residence in Drayton, in Northamptonshire. Not only is this conveniently located two days' ride north of London, but it was the place to which Keyes fled after the plot was discovered, and we have him secure.'

'If he has been taken, why did you make reference to him?' Francis asked. 'And surely, whatever he may have done is a matter best left to the Derbyshire bailiff?'

Emerson sighed again, then looked at Edward with an expression of sympathy, being professionally tied as he was to an idiot. 'He had not lived in Staveley for some time, but was known to have cultivated friendships here in Nottingham, where he was educated. It is therefore likely that any treasonous stain he left behind him before travelling to London is to be found in this town, or perhaps its adjoining county, given that it borders Derbyshire.'

'So you wish us to explore that possibility?' Edward asked.

'Yes,' said Emerson. 'At least one of you seems to grasp the realities here, the Lord be praised.'

'And what of our normal duties in the meantime?'

'Your employers will soon receive word directly from London that you are to be engaged full-time on investigations initiated by the attorney general. This will protect you from any accusations of dereliction of duty, but you might be best advised to meet with your sheriffs in order to make arrangements for your regular duties to be performed by others.'

'It might be a good idea for us to meet with all three of them at the same time,' Edward suggested.

Emerson raised his eyebrows. '*Three* of them, you say? Should that not be two?'

Edward shook his head. 'Nottingham has two sheriffs who share the office, not always very amicably. I'm sure that there are other towns with a similar arrangement.'

'No doubt,' Emerson conceded, 'but however many of them you are answerable to, lose no time in meeting with them. The last thing we need is an all-out war between the attorney general and the Lord Chancellor regarding allocation of manpower. And now I must take my leave; which is the best road for Lincoln from here?'

After he'd departed, Edward moved back into his seat behind his desk and Francis cursed.

'We've been taken off our normal duties, given an impossible set of tasks, forced to meet with our employers, and had our lives turned upside down,' he complained. 'I could do without this latest mission!'

'We're part of the way there already,' Edward assured him.

'I admire your faith, but doubt your wisdom,' Francis grumbled. 'Go on — persuade me.'

'Think back to our conversation with Will Bestwood, the current landlord of The Pilgrim,' Edward began. 'He told us about Tom Whitely's brother, who was educated here in Nottingham, where he fell into Catholic ways under the influence of his schoolmaster. He might have been describing this Robert Keyes from Staveley. And weren't we also told that the Whitelys originally came from somewhere on the Derbyshire border — Skegby, wasn't that the place? I'd be willing to wager that the Whitely and Keyes families were reasonably close neighbours, depending on where exactly Staveley is located. Even if they weren't, Robert Whitely and Robert Keyes could have been at the same school at the same time. And even if *that's* not the case, then the chances are that the Catholic schoolmaster corrupted them both.'

'So you suggest that we begin there?' Francis concluded with apparent reluctance.

'I most certainly do,' said Edward. 'You can make enquiries in Skegby, since it's within your jurisdiction, while I investigate the circumstances of the fire that was almost certainly the result of a misadventure with gunpowder. And while I remember, let's not overlook the known connection between that rear corridor in The Pilgrim and the dungeon passages in the castle. If you were intent on invading the fortress by stealth, or running barrels of gunpowder inside it ahead of blowing the place up, what better route than by way of the alehouse conveniently located at the foot of the castle rock?'

'When do we meet with our sheriffs?' Francis asked with a grimace.

'Without delay, if we are to convince them that we are doing our job.'

'And when do *you* intend to tell Kitty what you've got me into *this* time?'

'Why should I need to?'

'She is currently placing all the blame for my lengthy absences on me. It's high time she learned who the true culprit is. And now you owe me supper, I believe, before I set off back to Daybrook for another earful of complaints.'

Sheriffs Freeman and Gamble, joint office holders for the town of Nottingham, had needed little persuasion to leave their townhouses to make the relatively short journey north into the village of Bulwell, where they had dinner with their counterpart in the county, William Sutton. Francis and Edward were not invited to that dinner, but they were the official excuse for it, and would make it acceptable for Sutton to seek reimbursement from the Lord Chancellor's Office for the outlay.

It was now three days since the visit from Walter Emerson, and all three office holders under the Crown had received the disturbing advice that their bailiffs would, for the time being at least, be excused normal duties while they conducted a joint search for traitors.

'Is this connected in some way with that disgraceful attempt to assassinate His Majesty?' Freeman demanded of Edward and Francis. The three sheriffs were seated at a table in the former manor house that William Sutton had recently purchased, and the two bailiffs stood before them.

Edward felt obliged to reply, since Freeman was his employer. 'It is indeed, sir,' he confirmed. 'There is reason to believe that plans were laid for the taking of Nottingham Castle following the rebellion in London, which fortunately did not materialise. We have been sent in search of those who might have been involved in that aspect of the overall plot.'

'They must surely have fled by now?' Sheriff Gamble suggested, not wishing to be considered any lesser in authority than Sheriff Freeman.

'Not if they were local men,' Edward countered. 'Where better to hide than in plain sight, in the bosom of one's family, as if one had never been complicit in treason?'

'And it is being suggested that some of these malfeasors might be from the county?' Sutton asked.

This time, it was Francis who obliged. 'Indeed, sir. There is a possible connection with Skegby that needs to be investigated, and in due course it might be necessary to join forces with our Derbyshire counterparts.'

'How long will you both be absent from duty?' Freeman demanded.

'Absent from *customary* duties only,' Edward replied, 'but for how long, it's impossible to tell. However, my senior constable — Jack Durward — is more than up to the task of supervising all routine matters such as emptying the alehouses and breaking up fights.'

'And should something other than "routine" occur, what then?' Gamble asked grumpily.

'Then I shall do my utmost to deal with that myself,' Edward assured him with more confidence than he felt.

'Like that fire in Halifax Lane that rumour has it was deliberately lit?' Freeman demanded.

'As it transpires, that may well prove to be part of these new enquiries that we have been commissioned to undertake.'

'But what of the county?' Sutton asked petulantly. 'There is no senior constable to deputise for you, is there, Barton?'

'No, sir, but my wife will be able to take messages from anyone seeking to impart intelligence of any serious crime. And of course my network of local constables will remain in place in order to dispense justice at a local level — cracking skulls, consigning drunks to lock-ups, intervening in brawls and suchlike.'

'I'm sure I speak for all three of us when I express my extreme dissatisfaction with the proposed new arrangement,' Freeman bleated, 'but we acknowledge that you have as little control over orders that come from London as we do. Just see to it that you are able to intervene when it matters. You may now proceed with your allotted duties while we continue to discuss weightier matters.'

The two bailiffs made their way to the small stables and mounted their horses.

'That could have gone a lot worse,' said Edward.

Francis snorted as he patted his mare, Sally. 'The worst is yet to come for you, my good friend and dangerous colleague. You are invited to supper at Daybrook. And according to my good lady wife, the roast will be you.'

5

Edward reflected gloomily on the evening that he'd spent with Francis and his family.

Kitty had made her displeasure known as soon as Edward had taken a seat at the supper table. 'So once again I have you to thank for the loss of a husband?' she demanded as she slammed a plate of cold meats down on the trestle.

'He's not exactly "lost",' Edward replied. 'You must appreciate that as bailiffs, we are subject to orders from on high that…'

'I've heard that excuse so often that I almost think you believe it yourselves, but another way of looking at it is that you're both too weak to tell those allegedly in authority where to stick their orders.'

'It's not that simple…' Edward attempted.

'And neither am I!' Kitty snapped. 'Either you two are pathetic people-pleasers who doff your caps every time someone with an important title tells you to jump at their every whim, or you are pleasure-seekers pretending to be family men who use each other as an excuse to slip away in search of a good time.'

'That's outrageous!' Edward protested as he rose from his seat and threw his napkin down on the table. 'We serve the nation, keep communities safe, risk our lives daily in order to combat evil in all its many forms, and rue every minute that we are away from the comforts of home! We skulk behind hedges, squat in ditches, hide in derelict buildings in the depths of winter in order to catch thieves at work, and brave punches and kicks when we seek to suppress the violence of others, and *you* have the cheek to call us cowards and libertines! I will not take supper at the table of one who insults my office in that way!'

'Sit down and enjoy your supper, Edward,' Rose said softly from the other side of the table. 'My sister doesn't really mean all those angry words — she just worries herself to distraction every time you and Francis are called upon to work together, because it usually means that whatever you're engaged upon is even more dangerous than your usual duties. And as for you, little sister, remember how Francis came to be here in the first place — by helping me escape from accusations of witchcraft and almost certain death. You are married to one of the bravest and most honourable men who ever lived, and he loves you deeply and sincerely. He does not deserve your insults, and neither does poor Edward, who is about to forgive you and resume his seat. Are you not, Edward?'

Somewhat shamefacedly, Edward did as instructed and reached for more bread. Kitty could be heard taking deep breaths before she finally said, 'I'll apologise to Edward — and perhaps even Francis — if someone could explain why they're being sent to smoke out men armed with gunpowder and pistols who nearly succeeded in killing the king.'

'All those are now safely locked away in the Tower,' Edward replied, mentally seeking God's forgiveness for what might well have been a lie. 'Our task is simply to identify others of lesser rank who may have been assisting them.'

'Like those who blew up that house in the town?' Kitty challenged him. 'Francis tells me that three houses finished up as ashes, and that there were bodies littering the street.'

'We believe that to have been accidental,' Edward replied as reassuringly as he could. 'The house in question was, we believe, being used to store gunpowder that was destined for the castle. But such a plot would require several people to assist, and it is those that we seek. They have almost certainly gone into hiding, and we must identify them and hand them over to others.'

'Why does Francis insist that he must travel to Skegby?' Rose asked. 'When I was living in Linby, Skegby was known to be the haunt of ne'er-do-wells and people with no respect for authority. Will Francis be required to expose himself to low-lives like that on his own, or will you ride with him?'

'Sadly I will not,' Edward replied reluctantly, anxious to be as truthful as diplomacy allowed. 'I am already several days behind with my investigations in the town.'

'So Francis will at least be returning home each evening?' Kitty asked hopefully, as her face lost some of its anger. 'You will not be dragging him into town with you?'

'Not at this stage, no,' he replied.

Kitty looked him hard in the eye. 'How does Elizabeth feel about all this? Surely she must have protested in much the same way as I did a moment ago regarding the perils that come with your office. Was I being so unreasonable?'

'No, you were not,' Edward conceded, 'but she at least has learned to accept that this is the way I choose to provide for my family. I was a bailiff when we first met, and as events transpired she became well aware of the nature of my work before she agreed to become my wife. If I were a stonemason, a tanner or a fuller by trade I would be far less content with my life, and we would be living a more hazardous existence financially. And at least she has never called me weak, or pleasure-seeking.'

'For that I apologise most sincerely,' Kitty mumbled. 'I spoke out of anger, and I am fearful that one day you will take Francis on some mission and will be unable to bring him back.'

'If I know Edward,' Francis said nervously, 'it would be the other way round. Edward would never come home without me, because he'd die while trying to save me.'

'As would Francis for me,' Edward added.

'But who is to come to the aid of the *pair* of you, if you take on too deadly an opponent?' Rose asked quietly. 'For that eventuality, you will require those prayers that I offer nightly. So go in God's mercy, both of you, each to his allotted task.'

A short while later, Edward was mulling her words over as he trotted Oliver through the high hedges on either side of the lane that had just taken him through Woodthorpe on his way back into town. Suddenly, he heard a sharp crack that he knew only too well. He ducked instinctively as a pistol ball whizzed over the top of his bonnet and disappeared into the tangle of hawthorn to his left.

It was an automatic response to dig his boots into Oliver's sides in a silent command to flee the scene. The faithful horse almost succeeded in throwing Edward backwards out of the saddle as he lurched forward and began cantering along the dark and uneven surface. Edward reined him in a little, and as the canter became an urgent trot, he began thinking through the implications.

Someone had wanted him dead; that was beyond question. There were many who no doubt nursed that sentiment, but very few of them would be armed with a pistol — unless they were conspirators in a recent plot, anxious to avoid detection. But that raised an even more alarming thought.

Who else knew of the mission that had been handed to himself and Francis only three days previously, other than those who were ostensibly in charge of that mission? Did the conspiracy extend into the very heart of government? And were two innocent bailiffs being set up to fail?

Kitty had appeared somewhat mollified after Edward's departure, but the old look of resentment was back on her face the following morning as she walked out to where Francis was tightening his saddle leathers ahead of a two-hour ride towards the county's western borders at Skegby.

'I was planning on taking the last of this autumn's crop to Hucknall Market today,' she grumbled. 'They're starting to go rotten, but are still usable in pies and suchlike, so I'm hoping to get a few pounds for them. You can help me load them onto the cart before you ride off, shirking one duty for another, but what about at the other end?'

'Are you taking Richard with you?' Francis asked.

'Yes. It's easier than trying to persuade him to stay back here and behave himself. He's got *so* much energy these days, and he's grown quite beyond Rose's supervision.'

'Well, try engaging all that energy in something useful,' Francis suggested. 'I'm sure if you challenge him that he can't, he'll be only too pleased to prove that he *can* lift loaded barrels on and off a cart. And I have to leave now if I'm to reach Skegby, ask a few pertinent questions, then get back here for supper. I'd offer to ride with you as far as Hucknall, but I intend to take the quicker way along the Mansfield road, and I'll be trotting Sally the whole time. So good luck with the market, and I'll see you at sundown or thereabouts.'

'Make sure the "thereabouts" are not *too* late,' Kitty warned as she kissed him perfunctorily, then went back inside, calling for Richard.

It was noon by the time Francis hitched Sally to the rail outside The Wheatsheaf, on the Mansfield approach to Skegby. He walked into the all-purpose room in which a fire was burning brightly, and several customers were already occupying tables and supping pots of the local brew. He ordered bread and cheese, along with a large pot of ale, and casually asked the potboy if anyone locally could remember a family called Whitely.

'Who wants to know?' demanded a bleary-eyed woman as she raised her head from the table over which she'd been all but asleep. 'And what's it worth?'

'Another pot of that ale,' Francis replied as he took a seat on the bench across from her, 'if you can tell me what happened to them. I was at school with Tom Whitely in Nottingham, and he always used to tell me about his family's dairy farm here in Skegby. He and I often talked happily about the old days. Poor old Tom died recently, and I promised his brother-in-law Will Bestwood that I'd seek out any family that were left, because there might be some money to be distributed from the substantial estate that Tom left behind.'

'Is that right?' the woman asked eagerly. 'Well, what if I were to tell you that I'm his long-lost sister? What then?'

'I'd need some proof of that, obviously,' Francis replied guardedly. 'You could be lying.'

'And I *would* be,' the woman cackled. 'My name's Anne Saunders, and Tom was my uncle. That ain't good enough to share in the money, is it?'

'Probably not, although it will depend on whether or not there are any better claimants. For example, I'm told that Tom had a brother, who was presumably your father — were there any other brothers or sisters?'

'You needn't bother yourself about the brother. Robert, his name was, and he turned into a priest — one of those Catholic types. There's no way he'd have any children, is there? He was last heard of in prison in London, although in truth he was a lot nicer than bloody Tom, mean old man that he turned out to be. When my mam was left penniless after my father died, he

45

never lifted a finger to help us, so maybe he owes us something after all.'

'If you're Tom's niece, then there must have been another brother — is that right?' Francis asked hopefully.

At this point the potman brought over the ale that Francis had bought her, and Anne answered him after wiping the foam off her lips. 'Not a brother — a sister — my mam. Mary Whitely, she was, but the family threw her out when she got put inter shame by a man from over the border out Derbyshire way. That was my father, and he married her. Then he died, like I said, and Mam was left with me and my brother Jamie to bring up. But then she met this other man who'd been a friend of my father's, and he saw us right.'

Francis was beginning to lose the thread, and it showed in his face. Anne cackled mischievously and added, 'I've lost you completely, haven't I?'

'Not quite,' Francis insisted. 'Your mother took up with someone called Saunders when your natural father died?'

'No,' said Anne. 'Saunders was my father's name, and I kept it because it's better thought of around here than Keyes.'

Francis couldn't help showing his surprise and elation at having located his target so easily. 'The same Keyes family that live across the border in Staveley?'

'How come you know about them?' Anne demanded as all trace of humour left her face.

Francis thought quickly and forced a smile as he replied, 'Will Bestwood mentioned that there was a family connection, that's all.'

'Yes, well, it ain't one that it's safe to mention these days,' Anne muttered. 'One of that family's got himself arrested for treason, and he's down in the Tower, so it don't pay for me to mention that my mam took up with another of them — Ralph Keyes.'

'Is your mother still alive?'

'What's it to you, and why all these questions?' Anne asked, her eyes narrowing.

'Like I said,' Francis bluffed, 'Will Bestwood wants to know if any of Tom Whitely's family are out here. Now I can tell him that a woman called Anne Saunders is a niece of his, the daughter of his sister Mary.'

'Best that you say nothing,' Anne insisted. 'If it comes out that my mam took up with a Keyes, then we could be in big trouble. Promise to keep it to yourself?'

'Very well, if you insist,' Francis assured her as he made to leave, content with having acquired some useful information.

'You leaving so soon?' Anne asked as she rattled her ale pot suggestively. 'I thought we might get better acquainted, in a manner of speaking.'

Francis called for another pot of ale for Anne, left the money on the table, then bid her a polite farewell. As he left, he noticed a dark-haired, swarthy man getting up from the table beside Anne's. Perhaps he would take her up on her offer of company.

Ten minutes later, Francis sat on his horse, reflecting on his conversation with Anne. He'd just ferreted out a link between Tom Whitely — who may or may not have been assisting in efforts to smuggle gunpowder into Nottingham Castle as part of a plot to seize the fortress — and the Keyes family across the Derbyshire border, who had produced one of the principal conspirators in the attempt to blow up King James. He was pleased with his progress and, to judge by the position of the sun, he could be in Hucknall in time to help Kitty and Richard to load the hopefully empty barrels back onto the cart.

Kitty was all smiles as he dismounted, hitched Sally to the pole holding up the canvas over the market stall that she'd hired for the day, then gave her a kiss.

'The wanderer returns,' he greeted her, 'and with some valuable information that I need to share with Edward. How did Richard behave?'

'Very well,' Kitty replied, nodding in their son's direction. 'Not only was he able to assist in loading and unloading, but his cheeky manner entranced several ladies, who were persuaded to buy apples past their best in order to make wine or chutney. We've completely sold out, and we're over five pounds richer.'

'Well done, son,' Francis beamed at Richard. 'If you ask nicely, your mother may even give you a few pennies to spend at the sweetmeats stall.'

Richard looked pleadingly at his mother, who relented and held out two pennies. Richard grabbed them eagerly and raced off.

'You spoil him,' Kitty complained, 'and now he'll expect to be paid every time he comes with me to the markets.'

'He's worthy of being spoiled,' Francis replied. 'I'm used to seeing boys his age getting into all sorts of idle pursuits in the town, and sometimes even in the villages. Richard is so well bidden, but also intelligent and physically fit. There can't be many seven-year-olds with that combination of attributes. I have high hopes for him.'

'Well, since you let him slip away like that, the least you can do is help me load the empty barrels back onto the cart,' Kitty told him with a playful dig in the ribs. 'Then when he comes back with his ill-gotten gains, we can head home.'

They waited, seated on the tail of the wagon and chatting happily about their plans to clear another strip of their land in order to plant more saplings, until it occurred to them both that Richard should long since have returned from buying sweetmeats. Their anxiety deepened when Francis took himself off to the stall, only to be informed by an adjoining stallholder that the sweetmeat seller had sold all of her remaining stock an hour previously, then headed off early to her home in Arnold. Francis and Kitty consoled themselves with the thought that Richard must have gone in search of other treats to acquire with his twopence, but as the shadows lengthened, and more stallholders began packing up, their fears grew.

Finally, Kitty felt able to say out loud what she'd been telling herself for the past hour. 'Something's happened to him, hasn't it?'

'I don't know,' said Francis, 'but once darkness falls, he'll be even more vulnerable out here, alone in a strange town.'

'I should never have let you talk me into bringing him,' Kitty said accusingly, on the verge of tears, 'and I most *certainly* should not have let you persuade me to let him out of our sight. What do you intend to do about the horrible danger you've put him in?'

'I'll go and see the town constable and get a search organised,' said Francis as he leaped from the side of the wagon and strode off in search of Sandy Lane, where he knew the town constable, Jebediah Tomlin, had his residence. Fortunately Jeb was home, and Francis urged him to organise an immediate search party for Richard.

'He's probably just wandered off, like any young lad in a new place, fascinated by all the sights and sounds, particularly on market day. You don't have any reason to believe that someone might have a motive to take him away, do you?' Jeb asked.

Francis bit his lip. 'It's possible. I was in Skegby earlier today, asking some pertinent questions in relation to a serious matter that I'm investigating, and I got the feeling that I may have alerted the suspicions of the wrong people.'

'Any names you can give me?'

'Only one, really, since she was the only person I spoke to. A woman calling herself Anne Saunders.'

Jeb's face fell. 'A large woman with black hair sticking out in all directions, like she'd been dragged through a hedge?'

'That sounds like her, certainly,' Francis agreed. 'Do you know her?'

'Not just her, but the whole bloody Saunders family. They're a terror to all decent folk in Skegby. Thieving, robberies, a bit of prostitution now and then. If there's money in it, the Saunders lot is up for anything that's going. If you've crossed *them*, then maybe you *do* have reason to worry.'

6

The following morning Edward sat behind his desk, brooding and thinking. He'd not mentioned to Elizabeth that he'd been shot at on his way back from Daybrook. He didn't want to alarm her, or give her any further excuse to complain about the risks he was running by following orders from some shadowy official sent from Westminster. For all that Edward knew, Emerson could be a pretender — a man posing as a government official who was in fact sent by plotters in order to divert bailiffs and sheriffs from their proper functions.

But it was possible that there was someone else who was aware of the mission that Edward had been set. Someone who knew that he was visiting Francis in Daybrook in order to plan their next actions, and who might be aware of the route he was taking. The only person he could think of who knew such things was Elizabeth, but he didn't believe that his wife would betray him. Unless, of course, the plotters had some hold over her that she couldn't reveal, such as a threat against the children.

Edward shook his head vigorously and started to plan how he might learn more about what had led to Whitely's death, which might, in the end, turn out to have been a perfectly innocent accident. But could there ever be an accidental explanation, or indeed an innocent one, where gunpowder was involved? *Had* there been gunpowder in the house rented by the man calling himself Cuthbert, and what was he intending to use it for? If there was no gunpowder, how could one explain the explosion immediately before the fire that had been reported to his constables?

He still needed to interview those who might have witnessed something that had not been reported. On the other hand, blundering further into his investigations might expose him to reprisals from whoever had shot at him the previous evening. He needed a trusted and effective bodyguard, and one man sprang to mind immediately. Robbie Bishop.

Robbie was physically enormous and fiercely loyal to Edward, who'd taken him, as a youth, into his household service, thereby rescuing him from a lifetime of dull servitude in his father's carting business. Then, after Robbie had demonstrated his value when it came to brawling — and in order to give him a more steady income when he married local girl Mary Blythe — Edward had recruited him as a constable. He was the largest man under Edward's command, and the most feared by drunks when it came to suppressing alehouse fist fights.

Edward walked up to the front desk and asked the man on duty, Constable Mellows, if Robbie was on duty at that hour. When told that he was, Edward gave instruction that Robbie was to report to his room without delay. He had been seated in his office for a short while when his doorway darkened, and there stood Robbie.

Edward congratulated himself on his choice. The boy had grown into a man at least as tall as Edward, but much broader in the shoulder. His face was fleshy and resembled an undercooked turnip, and his mop of bright red hair acted as a warning to others that there was a quick temper lurking underneath. He was just the man to accompany Edward when he went back out on the streets with some penetrating questions.

He was about to explain Robbie's new duties when, to his surprise, the constable spoke first.

'I'm sorry it's come to this, sir. And after you've been so good to me, too.'

Edward felt a chill run up his spine as for one horrible moment he thought that his betrayer might have been one of his own men, and he hoarsely invited Robbie to clear his conscience of what was troubling him.

'That man that was living in the house that exploded, sir. It was me and my father who put the gunpowder in there. But we had no idea what it was, honest we didn't!'

Edward breathed more easily as he invited Robbie to bring in the bench from the hallway outside, sit on it and tell him the entire story. Robbie did as instructed, then sat twisting his hands in his lap as he explained.

'It was my day off, see, and Father had this big job he'd got from a man called Culbert. It was a big load, and my father ain't so young as he used to be, so I offered to help him. It took all day, because we had to go to an old cottage that this Culbert was living in, way out to the west of town. Then we had a full load of stuff to pull out of there, including two big barrels that were real heavy and smelled funny. Anyway, they were well nailed down, so we had no idea what was in them when we brought them into town and unloaded them at number six, Halifax Lane. We were well paid, and I thought no more of it until that fire I was called out to, along with the other men. I recognised the house, and when I saw the body lying there I recognised the man Culbert and all. I can only say I'm right sorry, and I never meant no harm, honest I didn't. Will I lose my job? Only Mary's expecting again, see — it'll be our fifth.'

'Not only will you not lose your job, but you've just earned yourself more commendation for your valuable work,' Edward assured Robbie. 'There was still some lingering doubt in my mind regarding whether or not there'd been gunpowder stored in that house when it went up in flames, accidentally or otherwise, but you've resolved that doubt. Do you by any chance recall exactly where you picked up those barrels from? Could you find that cottage again if I took you out there?'

Robbie shrugged, his face clouded by uncertainty. 'I remember we took the Mansfield road, then this man Culbert met us just as we were coming into a village called Ravenshead. He guided us into the wood where his cottage was. I reckon I might be able to find it again, if you give me enough time. Is it important?'

'It could be,' said Edward, 'but for the moment I want you to accompany me back to Halifax Lane. I need to talk to as many people as we can find who were there the night that the houses burned down. You probably know the locals there better than I do, but more to the point I need someone to guard my back. Someone took a pistol shot at me last night, while I was riding back from Daybrook.'

'If I see anyone trying to do that this morning, I'll rip their bloody arm off,' Robbie promised, and on that happy note they set off for Halifax Lane.

It looked different in daylight from the way Edward remembered it on the night of the fire, but the residual wreckage told its own tale. Numbers 5, 6 and 7 were completely missing from the row. Piles of ash, half-burned beams and general detritus littered the roadway, and Edward and Robbie were obliged to step round, and sometimes over, the mess as they made their way cautiously into the gap that was left. Then Robbie shouted at someone who was lurking behind the window of number 3, staring out at them with a look of fear on his face.

'Get out here, Jack Humbold!' he commanded. 'We can see you, and if you don't come out and talk to us, I'll come in there and drag you out by your skinny throat!'

'That's Jack Humbold,' Robbie told Edward unnecessarily as the man in question, an overweight and dishevelled individual in his late forties, stepped out and walked slowly towards them with his hands raised in supplication. When he was a few feet away he stopped, looking fearfully at Robbie.

'I've done nothing!' he protested.

Robbie gave a loud snort. 'Maybe not this time, but plenty of times in the past. This man's the biggest drunk in St Mary's,' he told Edward by way of introduction, 'and what he doesn't know about the goings-on of others ain't worth knowing. So start talking, Jack — where were you when that fire started the other night?'

'I was on my way home, after I got chucked out of The Dog and Bear for relieving myself on the floor,' Jack admitted, shamefaced. 'I stopped for another leak just about where you're standing, and the next thing I heard was a big bang. Two men come flying out of number six, taking the front wall with them. They were lying in the road where the constables found them, and number six was going like a bonfire in the marketplace at Goose Fair. Number seven was the next to go, because the wind was blowing the embers that way. I heard shouting and screaming from what must have been poor old Aggie Whitely and their daughter Kate, who lived there. Then the bloody roof came in on them, and I ran back to my house to wake the missus. We were standing outside, wondering what we could do to save our house from going the same way, when the constables arrived. I saw you there a bit later on, the pair of you,' he added, as if to give credibility to his version of events.

'So before the fire started you heard a loud bang, then the front wall of number six flew out, and two men were blown out by the blast — was that it?' Edward asked.

Jack nodded. 'Yeah — one of them was Tom Whitely, but he lived next door at number seven, so what he was doing inside number six I've no idea.'

'The other man who was blown out at the same time,' Edward pressed him, 'had you seen him before?'

'Sort of,' Jack replied. 'Number six was owned by Tom Whitely, and he rented it out from time to time. The man who finished up lying next to him out here in the lane was renting number six, but we hardly saw him. There was no reason to speak with him if we did see him, and he only seemed to come out at night. My missus saw him nailing shutters up at the windows when he first arrived. He was only here for a week or so — maybe less — before the place went up.'

'Did you ever see anyone else in number six?' Edward asked optimistically.

Humbold shrugged. 'Yeah — and no, so to speak. There were always shadows coming and going, but only at night time. I was usually on my way home late at night, and it was then that I saw them. I reckon they were men, because of the size of them, but I never got to see any faces. Just shadows, you know?'

'Yes, I understand,' Edward confirmed, 'but since you seem to be so well informed about local events, perhaps you can tell us about something else. There were only three bodies that came from number seven — the Whitely house — when it went up in flames. Were there any others residing there at the time, such as servants?'

'They had a maidservant — Lucy Buxton, if I remember right. She lived in a place out the back of there, next to the kitchen in the garden, but if she wasn't killed in the fire, then either she was sleeping in her quarters and escaped out the back, or she was out for the night. She's got a brother down Hockley way, and now that the house is gone she's got no work to come back to, so no wonder we ain't seen her since afore that night.'

'Nobody else?' Edward prompted him.

Jack frowned. 'There was that rogue that liked to call himself their steward, when he was nothing more than another servant. You could see him strutting round like he owned half the street, but it was rumoured that he'd been caught stealing by Whitely himself, and told to sling his hook. Wouldn't surprise me to learn that it was him what started the fire.'

'What was his name? And where would we be likely to find him?'

'He called himself Benjamin Tyler, but even that could've been a pretence,' said Jack. 'Can I go now?'

'Once you've told us where to find him,' Robbie snapped. 'Get the wool out of your ears — the bailiff asked you where he could be found.'

Jack seemed reluctant to reveal more, so Robbie leaned closer, gripped him by the throat and lifted him off the ground. He made a choking sound, then spat out, 'The Partridge, in Narrow Marsh! His father's the landlord down there, only don't mention my name, because it's one of the few places I can get a still drink these days.'

'No bloody wonder, if you relieve yourself on the floor,' Robbie said as he released his grip and pushed Jack away.

'Off you go — and thank you for your grudging assistance,' said Edward as Jack scuttled back to the safety of his own house. Edward looked back at Robbie. 'Who should we question next, do you think?'

'The girl Lucy?' Robbie suggested. 'If she was at the house the night it went up in flames, she might be able to tell us more about what happened just afore then.'

'How well do you know Hockley?' Edward asked.

'I know it well enough to know that there's a family called Buxton that runs a tannery down there. We get regular complaints about the smell, and from memory there's always a lot of youngsters hanging round the place. One of them might be Lucy.'

Edward nodded. 'It would certainly be preferable to wandering like helpless sheep into that wolf pound they call Narrow Marsh. Is it still hostile towards anyone who represents the law?'

'It is,' Robbie replied. 'We used to go there in twos — these days it's more like fours.'

'In that case, our decision's been made for us,' said Edward. 'Hockley, here we come.'

They could have found Buxton's Tannery just by the smell that drifted out from the narrow alleyway that led into its yard, but as it happened there was a sign that hung proudly above the front door of the modest cottage to the side. Edward knocked loudly. A weary-looking woman opened the door to them, then looked them up and down, as if selecting a joint of lamb at a market. When Edward announced that they were looking for Lucy Buxton, the woman jerked her head wordlessly to the side, indicating that they should make further enquiry down in the adjoining yard.

As they walked reluctantly towards the source of the smell, Robbie put a hand over his nose and mouth and told Edward how glad he was to be earning his living as a constable. 'Although some nights it gets as bad as this in some of the alehouses on the south side,' he admitted.

A heavy-set man sat gnawing on a bone, an ale pot by his side, as a young woman in her late teens or early twenties was swilling the ground behind him with water from a pail.

'A bit of a change from serving at the dinner table of the wealthy, is it not?' Edward asked by way of a conversation opener. When the woman looked back at him with raised eyebrows, he followed it up with, 'You *are* Lucy Buxton, are you not?'

'It wasn't me,' she insisted as she put down the pail and took two steps backwards.

'*What* wasn't you?' Robbie demanded.

She grimaced. 'That bloody fire. I was out visiting my brother, who lives here. This is him — Davey Buxton.'

'So when did you leave the house that day?' Edward asked.

She shrugged. 'Must have been about the middle of the day, after I'd served the dinner, and they were shouting at each other again. I was told to make myself scarce, so I did.'

'What were they arguing about?' Edward asked eagerly.

'The usual. The keys.'

'What keys?'

'Some keys to The Pilgrim. The master owned The Pilgrim — didn't you know?'

'Yes, I knew,' Edward confirmed. 'So why was he arguing with someone about the keys, and who was it?'

'The mistress. She was insisting that he shouldn't give them to the man who was staying next door, and he kept saying that if he didn't, his brother would stay in some gaol. I didn't really understand, but that's what they were always arguing about.'

'The man next door — what was his name?' Edward asked, just to be certain that he wasn't drawing the wrong conclusion.

'As far as I can recall, his name was Culvert, or something like that.'

'Could it have been Cuthbert, or Culbert?'

'Yeah, could have been, I suppose. I never really liked him, to be honest with you. He was always sneaking about, keeping his distance from everyone. Apart from Ben, that is — they were real close, him and Ben, and it was Ben who helped him nail up the shutters of his house. Then the master accused Ben of stealing from him, and he took off. Ain't seen him since.'

'This was Benjamin Tyler, the other house servant?' Edward asked.

Lucy nodded. 'Yeah, Ben, sneaky little bastard that he were.'

'What was he accused of stealing?'

'No idea, but the mistress was going on something fierce about it, and it was her who accused Ben of stealing in the first place. She insisted that the master throw him out. I think it was something to do with the keys again, but I couldn't be sure.'

'When did Ben leave the house?'

'It was the day before the fire. I remember because when I was told to take the rest of that day off, I thought that maybe they suspected I'd been involved in the stealing. The mistress was insisting that the master go next door and get back whatever Ben had stolen, and she told me that it'd be better if I wasn't around when he did that. *I* didn't steal anything, honest I didn't!'

'Don't worry, Lucy,' Edward said reassuringly. 'You're not suspected of anything. In fact, you've been a great help to us, and if I hear of anyone looking for a house servant I'll put in a good word for you. It's got to be better than swilling down a yard in a tannery.'

'Thanks. Can I get back to work now?'

After advising her that she could, Edward and Robbie made their way back down the yard and into the lane.

'Where to next?' Robbie asked eagerly.

Edward thought for a moment before replying, 'I think we should go back to the Guildhall and speak to Senior Constable Durward. If my suspicion is correct, we should shortly learn what happened to those keys that Lucy was referring to.'

They had barely entered the front hall of the Guildhall when there was swift movement from a seat to one side and Francis appeared before them.

'Edward, thank God!' he cried. 'I need your help urgently. Richard's disappeared, and I fear he may have been kidnapped!'

7

'You'd better come down to my room and give me all the information you can,' Edward urged as he gently led him towards the staircase, one arm around his shaking shoulders. He turned to Robbie Bishop. 'Bring me everything they took out of the ruins of number six.'

Robbie scuttled away as instructed, and Edward led Francis down the stairs, lowered him gently into the bench seat that had remained in his room since his earlier meeting with Robbie, then reached into his desk drawer for the brandy flask that he kept there. He insisted that Francis take a substantial swig of the restorative, and once he appeared to be coherent again, Edward asked him to describe what had happened.

'It was all my fault,' Francis admitted, his voice quivering with emotion. 'I suggested that Kitty take Richard to Hucknall Market with her, and when I got back there, after making some interesting discoveries in Skegby, it was I who suggested that Richard be allowed off on his own to buy some sweetmeats from a nearby stall. He didn't return, and when the market was eventually cleared of everyone who'd been there that day, there was no sign of him anywhere. I alerted the local constable, who roused a search party, and we all scoured the streets until well after darkness had fallen. We have no idea what could have happened to him, Kitty's beside herself, and I blame myself for blundering around in Skegby, obviously aggravating the wrong people, according to Constable Tomlin anyway. I must have been followed from Skegby, and they chose to pay me back by seizing Richard. He's only seven, and I fear that they won't even *think* to ask for a ransom, but may just do away with him.

I'm frightened for him, Edward, and I — I have only myself to blame, stupid oaf that I am!'

His face crumpled and he dropped his head into his hands, just as Robbie appeared in the doorway. Somewhat embarrassed, he looked down at Francis's heaving shoulders, then placed a calico sack down on Edward's desk.

'That's all of it, according to the senior constable,' he told Edward, who unsealed the bag and tipped its contents onto his desk. There were a few ornaments and pieces of crockery that had somehow escaped the inferno; then with a loud clatter and a shout of triumph from Edward, a set of three keys landed amid the rest. Edward picked them up and grinned at Robbie.

'Care to take a guess where they come from?' he challenged him.

Robbie nodded. 'They're probably the keys that Tom Whitely and his missus were arguing about, according to Lucy Buxton, anyroad.'

'Precisely,' Edward said triumphantly. 'Now ask yourself what those keys unlock, and how and why they came to be in number six, rather than number seven, where by rights they should have been, if I'm correct in my theory.'

'They must be the ones that man Benjamin Tyler's supposed to have thieved off Tom Whitely. As for what they unlock, you've lost me there.'

'Think!' Edward urged him. 'What else did Tom Whitely own, apart from the houses in Halifax Lane?'

'That alehouse — The Pilgrim?' Robbie ventured.

'Precisely! I bet if we were to go down to The Pilgrim and try out these keys, we'd learn that they fit every lock in that alehouse. In particular, a door at the end of the back corridor that leads up into the castle through a series of narrow tunnels.'

'I certainly remember those tunnels,' Francis recalled with a grimace, 'and there are still sleepless nights when I remember the black despair of being locked up inside an airless room with what looked like the remains of those who'd been thrown in there before me. It was Bailiff Mountsorrel here who rescued me,' he added for Robbie's benefit. His face fell. 'My fear is that poor little Richard's being held captive somewhere like that.'

'Clearly our highest priority is rescuing him,' Edward replied, 'but where do we start? There could be any number of places where they could hide him away — an old barn, a deserted cottage, an abandoned mill… Oh, wait a minute, though!'

Francis and Robbie gazed at him expectantly.

'You mentioned earlier that when you helped your father move all those possessions, including two barrels that were almost certainly full of gunpowder, into Halifax Lane for the man calling himself Culbert, from an old cottage. Is that correct?'

'Yeah, but I also said I'm not sure I could find it again,' Robbie reminded him.

'But you could try!' Edward persisted. 'It may well be where they decided to hide Richard for the time being, until they make their demands of us.'

'A ransom?' Francis asked.

'Possibly,' Edward replied, 'but perhaps they will instead demand that we cease our enquiries. We've clearly stirred something up out there in the county — someone took a pistol shot at me on my way back from Daybrook the other evening.'

'Let's hope we can find poor Richard before we venture any further, then,' said Francis miserably.

Edward fixed Robbie with a stern gaze as he asked, 'What was the name of the place where you were met by Culbert and guided to his cottage?'

'Ravenshead,' Robbie replied. 'It's way past Arnold, on the Mansfield road.'

'And how long after you met with the man did it take you to get to this cottage you mentioned?'

'Maybe half an hour,' Robbie recalled, 'but the pony was tired — we all were, and I wasn't paying much attention, to be honest with you.'

'No matter. It's as good a place to start as any,' Edward insisted. 'Go home, tell Mary that you won't be home for supper, then come straight back here with your pony. It's not long after the middle of the day, and we should make it to Ravenshead before nightfall, even at this time of year, when the days are short. Let's not waste any more time — off you go.'

Three hours later Robbie was apologising profusely for not knowing whether they'd turned right or left before actually reaching Ravenshead. Francis was getting more and more irritable as he watched the winter sun descending rapidly below the distant ramparts of Newstead Hall, off to their left. One lane led off to the right, in the direction of Blidworth, while a crude stone marker indicated that Papplewick might be reached by taking the track that led left, almost parallel to the direction in which they'd been travelling.

'I remember that the cottage was surrounded by lots of trees,' Robbie offered, 'and it looks like there are woods off there to the right, so maybe we should give that a go.'

Muttering darkly about the incompetence of town folk when left to their own devices, Francis kicked his horse's side and steered him into the narrow rutted path to the right, leaving

Edward and Robbie to follow on his heels. It was almost dark some thirty minutes later when Francis called a halt and nodded towards what looked like a broken-down former dwelling, framed by oaks and elms.

'Could that be it?' he asked.

Robbie shrugged. 'I can't be sure. Old cottages all look the same, and...'

'They all look the same to a town dunderhead like you, you mean!' Francis bellowed in his frustration. 'Thanks be to God that he blessed me with sensible men of ready wit to work under me in the county, and left the lackwits to Bailiff Mountsorrel!'

'Francis!' Edward admonished him. 'The man's doing his best, and we wouldn't have got this far if he hadn't had the wit to tell me about moving Culbert into town from somewhere round here. Thanks to Robbie, we can now be almost certain that there was gunpowder being stored in that house in Halifax Lane, which had been transferred from an abandoned cottage somewhere around here.'

'An abandoned cottage that this addlepate can't seem to find!' Francis replied, then froze when from some distance away he heard a faint voice.

'Father? Is that you, Father?'

The three men exchanged glances, as if they feared they might each be hearing things conjured by their eager imaginations. Then Francis called out, 'Richard — is that you? Where are you?'

'Hidden in these trees,' came the reply. 'Is it safe to come out?'

'Stay there, and we'll come and get you!' Edward shouted as the three men rapidly dismounted and ran through the coarse, narrow meadow that lay between the lane and the dense coppice. Then a flash of light-coloured clothing appeared between the trees to the front, and a boy some four feet in height came racing out to meet them. Francis gave a strangled cry of relief and scooped Richard up in his arms, hugging him tightly and asking if he was hurt.

'No, just hungry,' Richard complained.

'We can soon do something about that!' Francis promised as he took his son's hand and led him back to where their mounts were tied. He threw Richard in front of the saddle before climbing up behind him and nudging the horse back down the track for the return trip to Daybrook.

On the way back Richard explained how he'd found the sweetmeats stall empty, but had then been accosted by a man who'd told him where there was another stall further back, deeper in the rows of tradesmen's stalls. Then he'd been lifted off his feet and carried to a waiting cart, where another man helped the first one to tie him up, and drove the cart for what seemed like a long time. They eventually reached the cottage, from which Richard managed to escape. He hid in the trees, wondering what to do next. He'd been thinking of trying to find some friendly householder who might be prepared to feed him and show him the way home when he heard Francis's voice.

'He was shouting at me,' Robbie told him in a hurt tone, 'and it's perhaps as well I'm a dunce, else he wouldn't have been shouting, and you'd never have been found.'

'Yes, sorry about that,' Francis replied grudgingly, 'but as it turned out, we got lucky. Since you're a constable, I assume you weren't recruited because of your superior memory.'

'You're lucky he didn't demonstrate what he *was* recruited for,' Edward chuckled. 'You will recall that he took on those thugs who were guarding that jackdaw whose receiving house was being used to store and resell stolen property. Then he guarded our wives down in Ashby, while we went in search of that lot who were resentful of the king's accession. Robbie's the toughest constable I've got, and the most loyal, which is why he'll be staying in Daybrook for the foreseeable future.'

'What?' Robbie and Francis gasped in unison.

Edward explained his reasoning. 'First of all, whoever we're dealing with has left us in no doubt that we've got them on edge, and they've begun to fight back. I don't want your family exposed to further attacks while you help me to break up this latest ring of traitors, Francis. Kitty, Rose and the children already know Robbie from their time with him in Ashby, and no-one's likely to make any serious moves against them while Robbie's around the property.'

'But how long do you want me stuck out in Daybrook?' Robbie asked. 'And what do I tell Mary?'

'You don't tell her anything,' Edward insisted. 'I'll pay her a visit as soon as I get back into town, and tell her that you've been specially chosen for important duties in the county on a temporary basis, and will be getting an extra sixpence a day in pay.'

'And will I?' Robbie asked hopefully. When Edward assured him that he would, Robbie looked satisfied and remained silent for the rest of the journey.

It was pitch-black as they trotted down the lane towards the orchard, then turned into the long grassy track that led to the Barton family home. The front door was firmly shut and the house was in total darkness as Francis called gently for Kitty. He lifted Richard down from his horse and warned him to prepare for the hug of a lifetime, then instructed him to call for his mother.

The front door flew open, and Kitty appeared in a long nightdress that billowed out behind her as she rushed to pull Richard into her arms. She loudly blessed all the saints in a voice that cracked with relief as tears rolled down her face.

'It seems to me that it's Francis and Edward who deserve the praise,' said Rose as she appeared in the shadow of the open front door.

Once they were all inside the house, the rushlights were lit, and Rose rekindled the fire in order to heat up the potage. Then she rummaged in the bread box and produced the remains of a stale loaf that she placed in the centre of the table with mumbled apologies that she had nothing better to offer them. When Richard reached out eagerly and ripped a chunk from it, which he crammed into his mouth without any invitation, Kitty took him to task for his bad manners.

'The poor lad's been without food for a day,' Rose pointed out, 'and I've never seen anyone so keen to eat my stale bread.'

'You never told us how you managed to escape,' Francis reminded him.

It was Rose who supplied the answer as she looked across at Richard and asked, 'You climbed through a hole in the roof, didn't you?'

The lad looked surprised. 'Were you watching me?'

'In a sense, yes,' Rose replied as she reached out and tousled his hair lovingly. 'I believe I have what's called "the second sight", and sometimes when someone dear to me needs me, I can see where they are, and what the danger is.'

'We should have asked you first, before relying on Robbie here to take us on a tour of what seemed like the middle of nowhere,' Francis commented.

'It was Blidworth Bottoms,' Rose announced. 'I recognised it from the old days when I used to wander the countryside with my old donkey, selling simples and lifting imagined curses from the gullible. I'm not proud of some of the ruses that I performed in those days, and I give thanks to Edward every day for rescuing me from that life.'

'You also brought comfort to those who were sick in body and mind,' said Edward, 'so you have nothing to be ashamed of.'

'Did you also see how Richard managed to get his hands free?' Francis asked with a hint of sarcasm, but Richard himself was only too eager to explain.

'I used a trick you once taught me, Father. They'd only tied my hands with rope, so I looked for something sharp in the house, and found an old scythe blade. I rubbed the bit of the rope between my hands on it, and cut through. They hadn't tied my feet, so I waited until it was getting dark and I reckoned there was nobody outside, then I climbed onto an old table and punched a hole in the thatch. I always *was* a good climber.'

'A very resourceful young man who has an obvious career following in his father's footsteps,' said Edward.

Kitty let out a howl of protest. 'Don't you dare put such a stupid idea into the boy's head! It's bad enough having a husband who risks his neck every day for little reward, and who's never home. I suppose you're about to take him back into town with you, leaving us all defenceless here?' she demanded. 'The next one they kidnap may be me, remember!'

'They'd soon bring you back when you began haranguing them,' Francis chuckled, then ducked to avoid the wooden potage bowl that was thrown at his head. Fortunately it was empty, and as Rose retrieved it from the corner of the room and replaced it on the table with a frown in Kitty's direction, Edward took the opening that had just presented itself.

'You're probably wondering why Robbie's back in your midst. I'm leaving him here to guard the rest of you while I take Francis into town with me. He'll be gone for no more than a couple of days at a time, and Robbie can no doubt earn his keep around the orchard, or by teaching Richard self-defence in case anyone tries to kidnap him again.'

'Why do you need me in town?' Francis asked grumpily.

'You mean apart from the fact that I'm one constable down when I leave Robbie here?' Edward replied with raised eyebrows. 'Well, if you must know, I have two important calls to make, during which I'd find your company very comforting. The first is to The Pilgrim, which is under your jurisdiction anyway. The second involves a return to a place of which you will have many memories — Narrow Marsh.'

Francis groaned. 'I have memories of that pestilential place, certainly, but none of them are pleasant. Is it too late to resign my commission and just grow apples for a living?'

8

'You're far too late for breakfast,' Elizabeth told Edward and Francis frostily as they appeared through the scullery door of the Mountsorrel house in Whitefriars Lane. 'At least you had the decency to come in the back way, given all the muck on your boots. And I hope that Edward spent the night in Daybrook, and that the pair of you aren't appearing here in search of food after a night drinking ale somewhere.'

'I'm happy to cook something for Francis if he's hungry,' Margaret chipped in as she laid down her needlework and rose from her chair by the fireside. She smiled warmly at Francis.

'And how about cooking something for your father, while you're about it?' Edward asked.

'I suppose I can,' she agreed grudgingly, just as their maid Meg's face appeared in the scullery doorway.

'I hope I've not been dismissed,' she said, pouting. 'I was planning on serving fish for dinner today, since the fishmonger up at Weekday Cross had some fresh perch, and I was thinking of soaking it in beer afore cooking it on the griddle.'

'Sounds delicious,' said Edward, 'always assuming that there's any beer left by then. Francis and I need to talk for a while, after which we'll all be able to sit down to an early dinner. We'll be just by the back door.'

'In this weather?' Elizabeth demanded. 'It began to snow last night, while I was finally locking up the house that you left unattended, without any word as to where you might have gone. It didn't persist, thank Heaven, but it's still cold out there.'

'It certainly is when you live out in the garden,' Meg mumbled as she made her way out to the kitchen that was safely located in the rear garden, in case of fire. 'The beer barrel felt like it was half empty when I tried it this morning, so leave me enough for the dinner at least,' she added with a meaningful look at Edward and Francis as they followed her out.

'Meg seems to get cheekier every time I call in here,' Francis commented.

'She takes her lead from Elizabeth, unfortunately,' Edward replied ruefully. 'Anyway, let's pull those two benches out of the main room and sit here in the scullery, then you can tell me what led to reprisals after you travelled to Skegby the other day.'

'I enquired after the Whitely family,' Francis began, 'and almost immediately — perhaps suspiciously so, with hindsight — I found myself talking to some woman calling herself Anne Saunders, who for the price of a couple of pots of *very* indifferent ale claimed to be the niece of the late Tom Whitely. She only did so after I'd mentioned that there might be money coming to members of his family following his death, but she seemed to know already about the brother who went to the bad and became a Catholic priest. But the most promising thing that she revealed was that her stepfather was a member of the Keyes family, but that she was keeping quiet about it because one of them had been arrested in connection with that attempt on the king's life down in London.'

'Did she say whether or not this stepfather is still alive?'

'No, but I got the feeling that he may well be. Anyway, after Richard was kidnapped and I spoke with the local constable in Hucknall, he told me that the entire Saunders family have a reputation for all manner of wrongdoing. Thieving, mainly, but apparently they'll do anything for money, so maybe they were the ones who supplied that hiding place for the man Culbert that they later used to imprison Richard.'

'It's been a while since I was the county bailiff,' said Edward, 'but would I be right in remembering that Skegby's not too far from where we rescued Richard? And didn't we pass Newstead Hall on our way out there?'

'Yes, to both questions,' Francis confirmed, 'but so what?'

'You may have forgotten how Rose first came to Daybrook…' Edward began.

Francis raised a hand in protest. 'Of course I haven't. You found her living somewhere around Linby, and called me in to assist with removing her and her belongings down to where her widowed sister — now my wife — was living.'

'She'd actually been living in Papplewick when I first came across her, and it was from there that we removed all her belongings that day. You may not have noticed, but just as we were coming into Ravenshead, and were fortunate enough to turn right towards Blidworth Bottoms, we could, had we preferred, have turned left towards Papplewick.'

'This is all very interesting, Edward, but where is all this leading?'

'Rose is very familiar with the area in which those we are seeking may have been hiding. She will also no doubt remember much regarding the histories and family connections of those residing in the general vicinity of Skegby, which your Hucknall constable has already identified as a place that harbours the low sort.'

'Why didn't you mention this last night at supper?'

'It hadn't occurred to me then, and you were all so busy welcoming Richard back home.'

'So do you think she'll be able to help us?'

'Probably, at least with the second half of what we have to unearth — namely where all these plotters are hiding out now.'

'And the first half…?'

'That involves confirming what I already suspect about recent events here in town. I believe that Tom Whitely refused, at the last minute, to hand the keys to The Pilgrim over to the man Culbert, who intended to run the gunpowder under the castle in preparation for seizing it in the rebels' name. The same man who I suspect is the "Cuthbert" who we are told resided at number 6 Halifax Lane. But then I think he bribed one of Whitely's servants — a man called Benjamin Tyler — to steal them for him. When Whitely found out what had happened, he went next door to remonstrate with Culbert, who produced a pistol and succeeded in blowing himself up, along with Whitely, causing the fire that destroyed three houses.'

'Have you spoken with this Tyler, and if so do you have him locked up under the Guildhall?'

'Not yet. But that's why, later today, we'll be taking a full contingent of town constables down into Narrow Marsh, in search of him. His father's the landlord of The Partridge.'

'And before that?'

'We'll return to The Pilgrim, to test out those keys that I left in my room in the Guildhall.'

'Two alehouses in one afternoon,' said Francis, smiling. 'I'd wager the first will be more welcoming than the second.'

'Was it the quality of the ale or my dazzling wit that drew you back here so quickly?' Will Bestwood asked as he looked up to see Edward and Francis at his counter, where pots of ale were being exchanged for coins at great speed by the two unsavoury individuals on either side of him.

'Actually, we were wondering if you had a spare set of keys,' Edward told him.

'I was only given this set,' Bestwood replied as he reached beneath his apron and produced a keyring with three keys on it. 'Why, were you thinking of volunteering to work here? If so, you'd need a good character reference from somebody who ain't to do with the law.'

'I've no doubt we could get a character reference of sorts for you by consulting with the magistrates,' Edward replied, 'but were you never told that there's a spare set of keys to this place?'

'No, I wasn't,' Bestwood insisted. 'If there's another set doing the rounds, then maybe I'd better take steps to improve security in here.'

'Rest assured that the other set is in safe hands,' Edward said coldly as he extracted the spare set from the pocket in his tunic. 'What I'd like to know is how *this* set finished up in the house next door to your brother-in-law's — the one rented by the man calling himself Cuthbert. You remember — the house that exploded, then went up in flames?'

'No bloody idea,' Bestwood growled, 'but no doubt you're about to tell me. And how can I be sure that they're the spare keys anyway? You could just be pulling my leg.'

'Well, let's compare the two sets, shall we?' Edward suggested as he placed the spare set on the counter, gesturing for Bestwood to do the same with his. A close examination of the two sets seemed to suggest that they were identical, and Edward offered to demonstrate that this was indeed the case by enquiring which of the three keys on Bestwood's ring was for the front door, and which the back door. Having been shown, Edward and Francis tested the spares on the doors in question, proved that they were indeed what they had been assuming they were, then returned to the service counter to advise the temporary landlord of that fact. Then Edward asked, 'What's this third key for?'

'No clue,' Bestwood muttered. 'It ain't for the barrel store, anyroad. That doesn't even have a door. So what are you suggesting?'

'We'll just make a quick tour of the establishment, then let you know,' Edward replied, as he nodded for Francis to accompany him. They strolled down the rear corridor and stopped in front of the curtain that hung at the end. Edward pulled back the curtain, looked carefully at the lock, then sighed with relief. 'The keyhole is partly rusted, and appears to be occupied by cobwebs.'

'That's in keeping with the general lack of cleanliness in here,' Francis commented.

Edward straightened his back and added, 'It also suggests that no key's been inserted in here for a while. Hopefully that means that Cuthbert never had time to roll any gunpowder into the castle. But let's just make one final check, shall we?'

Without further thought Edward inserted the key, unlocked the door, and pushed it open with his boot. It opened with a low grinding sound that betrayed its lack of use, further confirming Edward's theory that any threatened attack on the castle had been extinguished by the recent explosion and fire in Halifax Lane. He began to creep along the dusty, narrow upward corridor into the rapidly diminishing natural light until he realised that Francis was not following. He turned and walked back to where his old friend was standing, ashen-faced.

'I'm sorry, Edward,' Francis rasped, his throat dry, 'but I just can't force myself to go — to go back … *there.*'

Suddenly Edward remembered, and apologised to Francis profusely as he placed a comforting arm around his shoulder.

'It's not as if we need to investigate any further up there, anyway. It's beyond any reasonable doubt that the threat expired when Cuthbert did.'

Francis nodded, then turned away from the still open door and murmured, 'Let's do something more acceptable to me — like risking our necks in Narrow Marsh.'

They paused at the counter to tell Bestwood that for the time being the spare set of keys would be retained in the Guildhall.

'I'll know who to blame if anything goes missing,' he grumbled.

'If an outbreak of a dreadful malady of the stomach is reported in the town, we'll know that someone made use of the keys to sample your filthy ale,' Francis countered.

'Why do you continue to provoke him like that?' Edward asked as they made their way under the lee of the castle battlements. 'In my experience, alehouse proprietors are a most valuable source of information in some enquiries.'

'But not, presumably, an enquiry into the whereabouts of Benjamin Tyler?'

'Time will tell, but I doubt it,' Edward grimaced. 'First of all, let's go and collect some head-kickers to assist with our enquiries, shall we?'

There were groans and protestations all round as the Duty Watch were called back into the Guildhall and told that they were to accompany the two bailiffs into Narrow Marsh, a pestilential slum of long standing that sat on the south side of the town, overlooking the marshes that fringed the north bank of the River Leen. Those marshes gave the cramped, squalid tenements of Narrow Marsh a permanent dampness that attracted vermin and gave rise to rot, disease and foul odours. The unpopularity of the dwellings down there resulted in reduced rents, and reduced rents attracted those who lurked on the fringes of law-abiding society. The town constables were visibly unimpressed as Edward lined them all up in Barker Gate, ahead of their short but most likely eventful journey down the slope that led into the shambles on the town's edge.

'We're heading for The Partridge,' he told them, and received several muted groans in response. 'I need to speak to the son of the proprietor, one Benjamin Tyler, and my request to do so will have two predictable consequences. The first is that Benjamin Tyler will head for the rear door, which is why Bailiff Barton, along with Constables Fry and Burridge, will be waiting for him just outside. The second is that all Hell will break loose once we announce our arrival, so have your clubs at the ready, and don't hesitate to use them. We probably won't be making any arrests, but I'd like us all to come out of this in one piece.'

There were harsh cries from several of those draped around various items of furniture inside the taproom of The Partridge as the first of the constables became visible during the coordinated rush through the front door. Edward had barely announced who he was looking for when a tall youth with an unruly mop of dirty-looking fair hair shot out from behind the counter. He sprinted through the open door that led outside to the trench in which the customers were invited to empty their bladders at regular intervals. A few empty ale pots began sailing through the air, and as the constables closed in on those launching them the taproom became the venue for several prize-fights for which there were no obvious prizes.

Edward forced his way through the melee and emerged at the back of the establishment, where he saw two constables standing well back while Francis rained blows down upon the youth who had tried to make a hasty exit.

'What am I supposed to have done?' the youth gasped.

'Leave some breath inside him, Francis,' said Edward, 'since I wish him to be able to answer my questions in due course.'

'He kicked me in the groin!' Francis complained as he administered one final punch, and had the satisfaction of seeing his victim sink to the ground in a pool of his own vomit.

'Pull him back on his feet, and perhaps Bailiff Barton might want to step back as carefully as he can with his bruised groin,' Edward said. When the youth was back upright, swearing and writhing, Edward walked right up to him. 'I take it you're Benjamin Tyler? You're not going to be in any further trouble, provided that you can answer a few simple questions. Truthfully, that is.'

'It wasn't me who started that fire,' Tyler insisted with a defiant stare.

'Possibly not,' Edward confirmed, 'but it was because of a certain theft by you from your employer that the fire came about, was it not?'

'I don't know what you mean. You talking about the keys?'

'I am indeed. You stole them from your employer Tom Whitely, didn't you?'

'So what? The man's dead, and you can't be taking me up for thieving from a man who's dead, can you?'

'I most certainly can,' Edward told him, 'otherwise men wouldn't hang for robberies that involved the death of the victim, would they? But I'm prepared to proceed no further with any charge of theft against you — or indeed murder — provided you tell me why you stole those keys.'

'That man next door — Solly, he called himself — he offered me five sovereigns to bring him the keys, so I did.'

'So you took five sovereigns by way of a bribe to steal the keys — then what happened?'

'The master — Whitely — found out they were missing, and that little sneak Lucy who worked with me told him she'd seen me next door with Solly, and how I'd been boasting that I had some money to spend. Then the master and his wife had a big argument, and the master told me to leave. That was the day *afore* the fire, which weren't anything to do with me.'

'But the master went next door to try to get those keys back?'

'No idea — I was back here by then, and it wasn't until I heard about the fire that I reckoned I might be in trouble.'

'When you went next door with the keys, do you remember seeing anything unusual lying around the house?'

'What, the barrels, do you mean?'

'Yes, I do. What was in them?'

'No idea, honest. But they smelled funny, like a fire grate the morning after a fire. The lid was a bit loose on one of them, and I lifted it and saw all this black stuff, like dirty sawdust. Solly caught me looking and warned me to tell nobody what I'd seen, or else.'

'Do you know if this Solly had the use of a pistol?'

'If he did, I never saw one.'

'Very well. I think that answers all my questions,' Edward told him. 'You're not going to be charged with anything — not even kicking a bailiff in the plums, since he seems to have dealt out a punishment of his own. Just keep out of trouble in future.'

'Can I keep the five sovereigns?'

'You mean you haven't spent them already? That's a matter between you and your conscience, so far as I'm concerned. One final question — what did this Solly look like?'

Tyler thought for a moment, then replied, 'He had lots of black hair that came down over his tunic top, and a nose that looked like you could hang your bonnet on it. He wasn't very tall. But you saw his body after the fire, didn't you?'

Edward wrinkled his nose. 'I can only assume that you've never seen a body that's been in an explosion. Very well, we're done here, gentlemen,' he said, turning to his constables. 'Assuming that none of you has enough of a death wish to remain here for a pot of ale, it's back to the Guildhall.'

A short while later, Edward, Francis and their escorts were making their way slowly up Garner's Hill.

'You just set a very unfortunate precedent for allowing the local scum to kick officers of the law in the groin with impunity,' Francis complained.

Edward laughed. 'And *you* just set a precedent for mindless violence against someone who you had no intention of arresting.'

'I could have arrested him for his assault on me,' Francis argued.

Edward raised his hand for silence. 'Let's just hope that you didn't encourage similar behaviour by my constables.'

They re-entered the Guildhall to find that, far from being allowed to rest, the constables were running back out again with the stern instructions of Senior Constable Durward ringing their ears.

'Timber Hill, on the double! Take your clubs, and make sure you use them to good effect!'

He became aware of the return of Edward and Francis, and called out to his superior. 'While you were gone, a fight broke out in The Swan in Timber Hill. Something to do with two men arguing over a lass, but it got ugly when others started joining in, and pretty soon there was a proper riot going on.

There was nobody to stop it while you were all away, but thank God you're back! Hopefully they can put a stop to it afore one of the sheriffs hears about it.'

'One of them already has!' came a bellow from the doorway behind Edward and Francis, who turned to see Sheriff Gamble glaring at them. 'Downstairs, Mountsorrel, and explain yourself!'

'May I bring Bailiff Barton with me?' Edward asked.

Gamble nodded. 'May as well, since he can perhaps explain why he's got one of my constables wet-nursing his family up in Daybrook. Downstairs, both of you — now!'

Edward indicated for Sheriff Gamble to occupy the only chair in his room, while Edward and Francis stood upright in front of the desk, awaiting the storm.

'As you've already been advised,' Gamble thundered, 'a full-scale riot broke out earlier today in a low alehouse in Timber Hill. There were no town constables available to suppress it because you had all the men down in Narrow Marsh, making enquiries into some matter or other. What was it?'

'The matter of that explosion and fire in Halifax Lane. We believe it's connected to the treason we've been asked to look into,' Edward replied.

'And it took all six of the Day Watch to ask a few questions, did it?'

'We never venture down there alone, sir. We haven't for some years now. Your predecessor...'

'I don't give a damn what my predecessor may have ill-advisedly allowed,' Gamble replied as the veins in his neck began visibly throbbing above his lace ruff. 'You should not have left the town unguarded like that! *You* may have been given the authority to play little games on behalf of some minor minion in Westminster, but you had no right to engage the rest of your Watch in it. And as of this moment, even *you* have had that authority withdrawn.'

'By London, sir?'

'No, by *me*! You are employed by me to enforce the law in this town, and regardless of what additional duties may have been assigned to you by some acolyte allegedly in the service of the king, you are to place town duties first and foremost in your daily activities. Have I made that abundantly clear?'

'Yes, sir,' Edward replied through clenched teeth.

Gamble turned his baleful glare on Francis. 'Why is Constable Bishop in Daybrook, Barton?'

'He's guarding my family, sir,' Francis admitted. 'My young son was kidnapped by those who Bailiff Mountsorrel and I are seeking to identify on behalf of the attorney general. Fortunately, he escaped, but...'

'I want Bishop back on duty within the town by midday tomorrow, understand?' Gamble demanded.

Francis simply nodded.

'Very well,' Gamble concluded as he rose from behind the desk. 'Let's hear no more about imaginary plots cooked up by self-important officials in Westminster seeking to justify their privileged ranks. I shall inform Sheriff Freeman of my rulings when he returns from his family frivolities in Yorkshire. Also, Sheriff Sutton shall be advised of how his county bailiff has been distracted from his priorities. Now go about your proper duties — both of you.'

It fell silent after he'd swept out, and Francis turned to Edward with a shrug.

'I'd better lose no time in getting back to Daybrook and sending Robbie back here. But I need to think about the safety of my family, so, with considerable regret...'

'I understand, Francis,' Edward reassured him. 'But I'm also in a quandary regarding what I should do.'

'You don't intend to follow your sheriff's orders?'

'Not if they conflict with orders that come, however indirectly, from the king. I need to have Gamble's orders countermanded, and I can think of only one way to bring that about. I believe that Elizabeth is long overdue a family reunion in Ashby.'

9

'Why am I almost certain that either you need us all out of the way at my parents' house, or that you need to travel there for some reason connected with your duties?' Elizabeth asked cynically when Edward proposed that they take a trip down to Ashby.

'Because you know me too well,' he replied sheepishly. 'But let me put this another way: I need to travel to Ashby anyway, whether you accompany me or not, and you're always complaining that you don't see enough of your mother and father.'

'I'd like to go,' Margaret chirped. 'It gets very tedious here, day after day. I'd like to feed Grandfather's chickens, and run up and down the drive to Ashby Castle with Robert, because I always win.'

'When I finally beat you, the whole world will know,' Robert threatened, 'but I'd like to go down there as well. The trees are more fun to climb than the simple ones in our garden.'

'It would seem that my mind's been made up for me,' said Elizabeth, glancing affectionately at her two oldest children, 'but let it be noted that we're not simply bowing in acknowledgement of your duties, Edward. Not that I'm really all that interested, but why do you need to go to Ashby anyway? Presumably you'll disappear up to the big house once we get there, and we won't see you again until you decide that we need to return?'

'I need to speak with the Earl of Huntingdon, certainly,' Edward replied with a frown, 'and you can blame Sheriff Gamble for that. He's attempting, for reasons that raise certain suspicions in my mind, to prevent me carrying out the instructions I got from London.'

'And why would he do that?'

'If I knew that, I wouldn't need to travel down to Ashby, would I?' said Edward irritably. 'But I have to get his order to me countermanded by a higher authority, and the earl is my quickest line of communication with London. I could make the trip there and back in a couple of days, if you'd rather not come.'

'As it happens,' said Elizabeth, with a distant look in her eyes, 'I've been getting these unnerving dreams lately, in which I can see my mother standing at the door of the cottage with an anxious look on her face, and I know that it's me she's waiting for. If you believe in the power of dreams, then perhaps she needs me. Even if I'm imagining things, I still need to go down there, if only to reassure myself that there's nothing wrong. When do you suggest we set out?'

'Tomorrow at daybreak would perhaps be best,' said Edward. 'Meg can visit her family while we're away, and I can leave the town under the reliable management of Senior Constable Durward. Francis is back in Daybrook, so he can guard his own nest now that Robbie Bishop's been ordered back into town.'

The following afternoon, the family were approaching the grace-and-favour cottage that Elizabeth's parents, Edwin and Catherine Porter, had been granted after their retirement from years of dedicated service in the castle further up the drive.

Elizabeth frowned. 'It's well past the middle of the day, and Father normally has the front door wide open while he sits outside, making his wooden toys for the village children,' she observed nervously. 'But the house looks as if it's been abandoned. I hope all's well with them.'

The front door opened as the weary party halted their horse-drawn wagon. A defeated-looking Edwin Porter shakily walked out to meet them, and tears began to slide down his gaunt cheeks. 'God be blessed!' he called. 'It's a miracle. Your mother was right to place her trust in prayer.'

Elizabeth leapt down from the wagon and rushed to her father, who clasped her in his bony arms and began to sob like a child.

'What is it, Father?' Elizabeth asked in a wavering voice. 'Is it Mother? Is there some illness, or is she — well, is she still … *with us?*'

'She is,' Edwin replied through his tears, 'but not for much longer, according to the physician that the earl very kindly sent down from the castle. She has a canker in her breast, and she's been praying for weeks to be able to see you one last time. I was wondering if I should send a message to you, but…'

'You didn't need to, Father,' Elizabeth croaked. 'Mother's prayers were received, and we must thank God for his mercy and blessings. But take me to her now, please.'

Edward had been watching and listening from the front board of their wagon, and now he climbed down and began to assist the children down into the dusty lane.

'You'd better go and find some trees to climb, all of you,' he instructed Robert and Margaret. 'Take your brother and sister with you, and don't come into the house until I tell you it's time to do so.'

It was a miserable night for them all. Elizabeth spent the entire time kneeling beside her mother, who was lovingly wrapped up in blankets. Catherine grasped her daughter's hand and gave an occasional cry of pain. Elizabeth couldn't even be persuaded to leave Catherine's side to make them all a meal, but Margaret was easily prevailed upon to demonstrate her maturity, and the skills she'd acquired by watching Meg at work in the scullery and kitchen at home. Not that any of them seemed inclined to eat, as a cloud of misery and foreboding seemed to descend upon the simple two-roomed cottage with its sickroom to the rear. The sad and silent family sat in front of the open fireplace, into which Edward kept placing logs from the supply that Robert was chopping outside, eager to burn off some energy and to do something to help.

It was with a guilty sense of relief that Edward rode up the long drive to Ashby Castle the following morning and sought an audience with its current owner, Henry Hastings, Fifth Earl of Huntingdon. The earl gave immediate leave for Edward to be admitted into the heavily panelled main hall, where a fire blazed merrily and mugs of fortified wine, along with a tray of wafers, were laid out for the benefit of the visitor.

Edward wasted no time in announcing the reason for his urgent visit.

'I require word to be sent without delay to London, requesting that the attorney general, or whoever, issue an order to Sheriff Gamble of Nottingham that he is not to impede the enquiries I am conducting in the search for those who may have been complicit in a plot to overrun the castle there.'

Hastings raised his eyebrows as he asked, 'Why would the sheriff do that, when he received an order to the contrary from the same man who gave you your instructions?'

'I have a suspicion,' said Edward, frowning. 'But I should perhaps be grateful to Gamble in one sense; he has inadvertently confirmed that my enquiries thus far have been both fruitful and of considerable threat to those I seek to identify and hunt down.'

'Please tell me briefly the extent of those enquiries,' Hastings urged him as he topped up Edward's mug and slid the wafer plate closer to him.

Edward shook his head briefly in response to the gesture, then began. 'As you will no doubt have been advised by Master Emerson, there was recently an explosion and fire in a row of houses in one of the better streets of Nottingham. The blaze completely destroyed three of those houses and resulted in the death of a man called Thomas Whitely, who owned all three of those houses, his wife and child, and a somewhat shadowy character who'd been renting the house next door to Whitely. My enquiries have left me in no doubt that the cause of that fire was the accidental triggering of several barrels of gunpowder that were being stored in the rented house — gunpowder that had been intended for transfer into Nottingham Castle as part of a planned attack on its defences. The chosen route for the introduction of that gunpowder was, I believe, a series of tunnels that lead up into the castle from ground level at the rear of a low alehouse called The Pilgrim. This was owned at the time by the same Tom Whitely who died in the fire.'

'So, a bungled plot that failed due to the incompetence of the plotters,' Hastings summarised with satisfaction. 'A pity that this man Whitely is no longer available to be handed over to those in the Tower skilled in obtaining information. Were you able to follow the trail further outward towards those who might also have been complicit in it?'

'Indeed I was,' said Edward. 'Bailiff Barton, from Nottinghamshire, was sent out to a place called Skegby to make cautious enquiries into any family links that this man

Whitely might have had with others on the borders with Derbyshire. That county is the former dwelling place of one of those you already have in the Tower, Robert Keyes.'

'And was he successful?'

'He was a little *too* successful,' Edward confirmed. 'He began to ask questions that revealed a connection between the Keyes family of Staveley and the Whitely family in Nottingham, and soon after his son was abducted. Fortunately, he managed to escape, but the previous evening I was shot at as I rode back from Barton's home in Daybrook. I had learned from a former servant of Tom Whitely that the mysterious stranger who'd been renting the house next door had been anxious to acquire the spare set of keys to The Pilgrim. That, you will recall, is the alehouse through which access may be gained to the castle tunnels via a doorway at the end of the rear corridor, the key to which is one of those kept on the alehouse ring.'

'You have clearly begun to stir up unease among those who were involved in the plot,' Hastings agreed. 'And it is your belief that Sheriff Gamble is somehow seeking to hide his own complicity?'

'So it would seem,' said Edward. 'You might wish to get someone in London to investigate any contacts Gamble may have among those already suspected of involvement in the overall plot.'

'What about this "shadowy character" you referred to who was renting the house in which the explosion and fire occurred?' Hastings asked. 'Do you have any clearer idea of who he might have been?'

Edward shrugged. 'He's definitely something of a mystery. The only witnesses I have who actually met him can't even agree on his name. Some refer to him as "Cuthbert", or "Culvert", but the most likely name seems to be "Culbert". A man who dealt with him on a personal level — the man who eventually stole the spare set of keys for him — referred to him as "Solly". But that's all I have, although to judge by the expression on your face I may have struck a nerve.'

'You have. Could it have been "Calvert"?' Hastings asked.

'It sounds as likely as any of the others, certainly. Why, is that name known to you?'

'The name Solomon Calvert certainly is,' said Hastings as he took a long swig of wine. 'As his name suggests, Solomon Calvert is — or, according to what you now tell me, *was* — a Jew. His name kept cropping up whenever we were trying to penetrate the dark veil of intrigue that lay behind all the recent attempts by Catholics to undermine the reign of our current king.'

'And Calvert was assisting with these schemes?' Edward queried.

'He was assisting himself to riches and influence, more like. He was born into wealth, since his father was a very successful import and export merchant in the old city. To begin with, Solomon seems to have intended to follow in the same vein, until he experienced a substantial setback in fortunes when an investment he made in one of those recent speculative ventures into the New World went bad. He was left almost penniless. He managed to claw his way back up and eventually had even more wealth than his father had been able to boast. But he retained a deep resentment against both the Protestants who had launched the failed venture, and the officials under the late Queen Elizabeth who refused to punish those responsible — Solomon alleged that they had been dishonest.'

'So he went over to the Catholic side?'

Hastings shook his head. 'Hardly. But Calvert *was* seeking revenge, and an opportunity to make others pay for the years of penury and backbreaking effort that had been required in order to restore his fortunes. He was also, of course, committed to bringing down any Protestant or government organisation that, to his warped mind, he could blame for what had befallen him. He travelled regularly overseas, and was soon telling rebel or traitorous groups that he was prepared to fund any plot that would result in an end to what he saw as the self-satisfied and self-perpetuating clique that ruled England, regardless of whatever religion they followed.'

'When I was helping to bring down the last plot, it was believed that money had been promised from the Spanish Court,' Edward recalled. 'Various leading nobles, including Sir Walter Raleigh, were suspected of being the go-betweens. Are you telling me that the true go-between was in fact this man Calvert?'

Hastings shrugged. 'We are still investigating the extent to which Raleigh was involved, but given that his name is also associated with ventures into the New World, it's unlikely that Calvert would have been working with him. Another theory favoured by Sir Robert Cecil is that the money was to come directly from Calvert.'

Edward's face clouded with uncertainty. 'How did someone so high up in the conspiracy come to be skulking in a somewhat dreary house in a nondescript row in Nottingham, which is hardly the headquarters of power in this country?'

'Remember that those behind the latest plot scattered to various safe houses up and down the nation once one of the main actors — a man named "Fawkes" — was captured, and began giving us names. Calvert may well have been seeking simply to disappear from sight — to blend into the background, if you prefer. His offer to continue with the capture of Nottingham Castle was both an excuse and a means of saving his reputation while making himself invisible. His death — if it was in fact his — is a considerable blow to the plotters, but of very great benefit to those seeking to preserve the life of the king.'

'It's also a huge step backwards in my investigation,' Edward complained. 'I can hardly question a corpse regarding his recent contacts, and those who were his companions during those final days are now well hidden from sight.'

'You must find some way of flushing them back out into the open,' Hastings told him.

Edward frowned. 'I don't suppose you have any inspired ideas as to how I might achieve that?'

'You must identify something that motivates them strongly enough to reveal themselves,' Hastings told him. 'Something that they either desperately need, or desperately fear.'

Edward thought for a moment. 'The men, or possibly women, that I seek are Catholics steeped in the old beliefs, are they not?'

'In the main, yes, but how does that help you?'

'It means that they have both a fear of Hell and a belief in witches' curses,' said Edward.

Hastings snorted. 'Since you cannot personally consign them to Hell, and you are not a witch, how can you make use of those weaknesses?'

'I have an idea that might prove effective in at least identifying those we are seeking,' said Edward, 'but I will require assistance from London.'

'That will rather depend upon what you are going to ask for,' Hastings cautioned him.

There was a glint of determination in Edward's eye as he asked, 'Could it be said that King James persecutes witches because he fears them?'

'I would not say so openly, but yes, that would be a fair assumption.'

'So he believes in their power,' said Edward. 'That being the case, what if he were to have preserved the life of the most dangerous witch he'd ever encountered, in exchange for her placing a curse on all those who became involved in the latest plot against him?'

Hastings nodded. 'I could even believe that myself, but how would it assist you?'

'I know of a so-called wise woman who was accused of witchcraft several years ago, and narrowly escaped being hanged. In the area where she used to live, it is widely believed that she has the power to both cast and lift spells. If it is broadcast abroad that King James employed a powerful necromancer to curse those who plotted against him, then those who are guilty will come to her for the removal of the curse — for a charm bracelet or talisman, or whatever. This is how we may identify them!'

The expression on Hastings' face reflected his doubt. 'It sounds like a madcap scheme to me, but there can be no harm in trying it. I shall make arrangements for that rumour to circulate, and will also request that enquiries be made into the affairs of Sheriff Gamble, who hopefully will prove innocent of any involvement. For your part, do not cease your own independent enquiries into those possible family connections with Robert Keyes. And so I wish you God speed and good fortune.'

'You can hardly expect me to return with you, given the circumstances,' Elizabeth told Edward when he announced that he was returning north the following morning. 'I intend to stay with my mother until … well, until I'm no longer required, and even then I must see to Father's welfare. He will grieve sorely when she passes, and we can only hope that God is merciful towards her in her final hours.' Then the stern face that she'd been maintaining crumpled, and she sobbed helplessly on Edward's shoulder.

'I shall be journeying to Daybrook within the next few days,' Edward replied, 'and while there I shall seek some simple from Rose that will ease your mother's suffering. I shall then return with it, hopefully by the week's end.'

'Take care, Edward,' she pleaded. 'I know that your every working hour is beset with danger, but at this time more than any other I could not bear to lose you.'

'Have no fear. I shall return alive and well,' Edward assured her with more confidence than he felt.

10

Once back in Nottingham, Edward briefly visited his home and washed the grime of travel from himself. He then made his way to the house of Jack Mullard and his wife Kate, who was the sister of Edward's housemaid Meg. Jack was a stonemason only a year away from acquiring 'journeyman' status, and their house was in a modest row of workmen's cottages in Pepper Street in Sneinton. Edward was known by sight, and when she spotted him Kate put down the tub of wet washing that she'd been about to hang out in the communal green to the rear of the row. With a welcoming smile, she invited Edward to take a seat in the all-purpose room in which two children sat eyeing him with interest until Meg answered her sister's call and entered through the back door.

'Are you all back from Ashby?' she asked hopefully as she nodded towards her niece and nephew. 'Only those two are giving me a headache.'

'I'm the only one back at present, Meg,' Edward told her, 'because the mistress has been obliged to remain in Ashby, to bring comfort to her dying mother. It would be best if you remain here for the while, if only to silence wagging tongues while I'm at Whitefriars Lane on my own. But if you could see your way to ensuring that there's enough food in the larder to feed me once a day, that would be greatly appreciated. I anticipate being absent from the house as regularly as normal, and will take my other meals elsewhere.'

'Good news for the pie vendors,' Meg said, 'and any excuse to get away to the market for a few hours is a good one, I reckon. So do you want me to start back today?'

'That might be good,' Edward agreed, 'although I'll be travelling to Daybrook later today, and will probably bide there for a day or two, so you won't see me back straight away.'

'You'll likely be getting into more trouble with that friend of yours, Francis Barton,' Meg said. 'The mistress reckons he's a bad influence on you.'

'He's also the bailiff for the county,' Edward reminded her, 'so he's due some respect.'

Meg apologised in a subdued tone, and set about clearing the table in the centre of the room ahead of dinner. Edward politely declined to join the family for the meal, since he had to visit Warser Gate before he could head off for Daybrook.

His second destination that morning was a similar cottage a few lanes away that was seemingly overflowing with the four children who raced out to meet him as he dismounted, and surrounded his horse in the hope of being invited to ride it. They were called back sharply by a large lady who was clearly expecting her fifth child. She smiled affectionately as she recognised their visitor.

'Are you taking Robbie away again?' she asked eagerly. 'If so, you'll be doing me a favour, afore he eats us out of house and home.'

Edward chuckled with delight at seeing Mary obviously so contented with life. Throughout her early life, she had been exploited by a group of housebreakers and murderers, but she'd settled down once Edward had rescued her as a key witness to the innocence of Francis, who'd been wrongly charged with the murder of Mary's lover at the time. She and Robbie Bishop had subsequently fallen for each other, and four children later they were the perfect happy couple.

Feeling a gnawing sense of guilt regarding what he had to do, Edward waited until Robbie appeared in the doorway behind

Mary. 'I'm on nights this week,' he said. 'Is it something special?'

'It's certainly something special, Robbie,' Edward assured him. 'You're going back to Daybrook.'

'I've only just come back from there,' Robbie reminded him. 'What is it this time?'

'Something that requires your talent for looking threatening,' Edward said. 'I'm afraid that you may be away for a while.'

'Mary's due to give birth in the spring, they reckon,' Robbie told him with a nod towards Mary's swollen stomach.

'You probably won't be away for that long,' said Edward, 'but you may be able to return with that lovely wise-woman you helped to guard in Ashby a few years ago. She's the best person in the whole of the county to have at a lying-in.'

'Off you go then, Robbie,' Mary urged him. 'What you started you can help finish.'

Francis's children ran out to meet them as they trotted the final few yards to the house in Daybrook. Richard solemnly took the horses' reins from both visitors and led their mounts towards the stables at the end of the fruit barn, while little Amy, not yet three years old, giggled with delight as Robbie scooped her off the ground and swung her high in the air.

'It must be suppertime,' Francis said from the doorway, 'but the appearance of Robbie Bishop suggests that we're about to go looking for a house he can't quite locate.'

Robbie glowered at the gibe, but he was rescued by Kitty, who appeared in the doorway behind Francis. 'Leave the lad alone!' she said. 'He helped to rescue Richard, and he can lift apple barrels twice as well as you can!'

Rose joined her and smiled when she saw who had returned, adding, 'And at least he appreciates my chutney. Do come in, both of you, and I'll organise some supper.'

'This is presumably not a social call,' Francis observed as he selected some cheese from the platter on the table.

'Before you descend into talk of your many duties,' Rose interrupted, 'how are Elizabeth and your family?'

'I went down to Ashby, and my immediate family are well, thank you. But sadly Elizabeth's mother has a canker of the breast, and is not long for this world.'

'Does she suffer?' Rose asked. 'If so, I can soon arrange to be at her bedside with some soothing simples.'

'I would certainly be obliged if you could supply me with simples that will ease her pain. But I have another request to make of you that would prevent your journeying to Ashby.' It fell silent as everyone waited for him to continue, and he turned to bring Francis up to date. 'I managed to speak with the Earl of Huntingdon, and he, among other things, has agreed to countermand Sheriff Gamble's instruction that we cease investigations.'

'I'm still awaiting the same instruction from Sheriff Sutton,' Francis told him, 'but then we rarely see him out here. He may as well be in the Americas for all that we see him on our doorstep. He always requires me to travel to him.'

'Well, be that as it may,' Edward continued, 'I for one was at a loss to know where to continue our enquiries, given that the man we could have handed over for questioning died in that explosion and fire. His actual name was Solomon Calvert, by the way, and according to the earl he was the mastermind behind much of the plotting against the king in recent years. So in that sense his death is a blessing, but that still leaves us with a dead end.'

'Unless you count the Saunders family,' Francis reminded him, provoking a snort from Rose.

'Francis told me all about them, and if there's any remaining villainy to be performed, they'll be the first in line.'

'Do you know them well?' Edward asked hopefully.

'I only know *of* them, and if ever a family was cursed with an evil reputation, it's that one.'

'Funny that you should mention curses,' said Edward, 'because I arranged for one to be cast while I was in Ashby.' Everyone turned to stare at him. 'As matters stand,' he continued, 'we may *believe* that we know who else in the town or county may have been implicated in what they are now calling the "Gunpowder Plot", but we have no positive proof. We must therefore devise some strategy for obliging them to identify themselves, which is where Rose will be of such value to us. And Robbie, of course, since he will be working alongside Rose.'

'If he couldn't even find a house he'd visited a week or so previously, how can he assist with identifying those who are working so hard to keep their identities hidden?' Francis asked.

Edward cast an anxious glance at Robbie's darkening countenance, then replied, 'Francis, if you're not prepared to listen to your wife and sister-in-law when they tell you to cease goading Robbie, then let me remind you of his ability to fight two men at once, each of them much tougher than you.'

'I'll let it go, honest I will, sir,' Robbie assured him.

Rose placed her hand on his sleeve. 'You have such a sweet nature under all that muscle, Robbie. You are the ideal man — strong but sweet-tempered. You will enjoy a long life, and will be adored by your wife and six children.'

'I've only got four, with one more on the way,' Robbie objected.

Rose squeezed his arm. 'There will be a sixth, and both it and the one about to come will be boys.'

Robbie's mouth dropped open, and Edward hastened to fill the silence with an explanation.

'Rose is a wise-woman, Robbie, and I've never known her to be wrong. But she's going to need your protection, if she agrees to my proposal.'

The silence continued, so Edward chose this moment to trade in a long-standing favour as he turned to Rose.

'Do you recall, when we first met, that you were living in a crude hut on a riverbank in Papplewick, and the master of Newstead, who was the county sheriff at the time, sent me to arrest you for witchcraft?'

'Of course I do,' said Rose. 'I owe you my life for not having carried out that order. Instead you escorted me here to Daybrook, to be reunited with Kitty. Where is this leading?'

'Well, when we got talking on that first occasion, you admitted that you'd earned a living for a while by selling amulets or charm bracelets to men who were working on the restoration of Newstead Hall — or Newstead Abbey, as it had been before the Dissolution. You said they had been frightened by tales of a ghostly monk who haunted the former abbey grounds, and resented the changes.'

'I don't deny any of that,' Rose replied, 'so kindly get to your point.'

'My point is this: you had a reputation for being able to lift curses and ward off evil spirits, and I wish you to resume that trade.'

Rose's face reddened. 'It was *not* a "trade", as you call it. It was a wonderful gift that was granted to me, and which I may only use for good.'

'Really?' Edward challenged her. 'All those charms that you sold to the gullible — they *really* warded off evil spirits, did they?'

'No,' Rose replied coldly. 'As I told you at the time, they simply served to relieve those who bought them of any *fear* of evil spirits. Such beings feed on human fear — if you do not fear them, they cannot assail you.'

'But for whatever reason, those who sought your assistance believed in your powers,' Edward persisted. 'While in Ashby, I persuaded the earl to make arrangements with his masters in London to put about a false rumour that King James, in retaliation against those who had sought to destroy him, pardoned a powerful witch in exchange for her cursing all those who had been involved. The guilty parties will naturally believe that they have been cursed, and will seek out a wise-woman in a desperate attempt to lift that curse.'

'You mean me?' Rose asked quietly.

'Indeed you. You will go back into the general vicinity of Papplewick, where you will be remembered, and wait for the queue to form outside your door. You will insist that the curse cannot be lifted except by some fancy ritual that involves invoking the name of the person from whom the curse is to be lifted. Then you simply report the names to me, or to Francis. When we believe that we have them all, we will move in with a company of men at arms and apprehend them all at once.'

'I have thus far remained silent,' Kitty chimed in tersely, 'but I can no longer sit idly by while you persuade my sister to place her life in peril. These people are evil, Edward, and one breath of her real purpose in such a harebrained scheme will get her killed.'

'Two points,' Edward replied calmly. 'The first is that if those we are seeking to flush out believe sufficiently in Rose's powers to seek her assistance, they are hardly likely to risk their own necks by laying hands on her. Secondly, Robbie will be with her at all times.'

Robbie and Rose exchanged puzzled looks.

'I could hardly claim that he's my paramour, given the difference in our ages,' Rose objected. 'My grey hair is rapidly becoming white — in fact, I have no doubt that it is turning whiter as we speak, at the mere thought of exposing myself to these evil people.'

'The age difference could make him your son, could it not?' Edward countered.

'Of course, but how could we explain away the fact that I lived for many years in Papplewick without anyone ever seeing me with a child?' Rose asked.

'I have the perfect story worked out,' said Edward.

Kitty groaned and Francis gave a cluck of disapproval. 'I have no doubt that you have, Edward,' he said, 'but it had better be a good one.'

'It is,' Edward insisted. 'While travelling in the Newstead area, and before she took up residence in Papplewick, Rose met a travelling man with whom she took to the road for a brief while, during which time they had a child together. Then one night, her man — let's call him "Robert of Leicester" — abandoned her, taking the child with him. Rose grieved her loss for many years, then only last year she was urged by an inner voice to search for her long-lost child in Leicestershire. She was journeying through a village called Quorndon when she was drawn to a roadside inn, at which this young man was working as a potman. A light over his head revealed him to be her child, who'd been abandoned in a nearby village called Mountsorrel and taken to a Leicester orphanage by a local clergyman who found him in a doorway. When old enough, he was sent out into the world, and served as a soldier before being discharged from Her Majesty's service. He wandered back to the only area of the country that he knew, and there he was found by Rose.'

'That's a very impressive story,' Kitty conceded as she wiped a tear from her eye.

Francis gave a dismissive snort. 'It's no invention, is it, Edward? It's basically *your* life story.'

'Elements of it, certainly,' Edward admitted. 'Good enough to persuade the curious, anyway.'

'Where do you propose that Robbie and I take up our residence?' Rose asked. 'Do I have to construct another hut by a riverbank?'

'It just so happens that Robbie knows where there's an abandoned cottage in Blidworth Bottoms,' said Edward.

Francis laughed. 'If he can find it this time.'

'I can find it,' Robbie growled, 'and that's the last time you'll get away with that jest without getting a bloody nose.'

'So are we agreed?' Edward asked before Francis got himself flattened.

Rose nodded, then looked across at Robbie as she asked, 'Do you promise to take good care of your old mother, Robbie?'

'I do if she keeps cooking all those lovely meals,' he replied. Then he looked enquiringly at Edward. 'Do you want me to come and let you know when somebody's asked for the curse to be lifted?'

'Not every time,' Edward replied, 'since whenever you call back here, you'll run the risk of being followed, and then our ruse will be revealed. Just make a note of all the names you collect, then bring Rose back here when you believe you've got them all — say, after two weeks in which you've received no new callers.'

'What do you propose that I do in the meantime?' Francis asked.

'Your normal duties, as if nothing had changed. You might even consider spreading the rumour of the curse in a casual way.'

'And what will you be doing?' Kitty asked of Edward.

'If Rose would be so kind as to prepare a few simples, I'll return to Ashby, first of all to confirm that the pretended curse has been launched, and secondly to provide Elizabeth's mother with some relief from her sufferings. I suppose I should also show my face again in the town, to see whether or not Sheriff Gamble's demand for me to cease investigations has been countermanded by London. We must also assume that Francis never was so constrained, since from what he tells me he's heard nothing from his sheriff.'

That state of affairs changed the following morning, after a lengthy breakfast during which everyone rehearsed the roles they were to play. They were about to move out into the front yard and load the spare wagon that would carry all the items Rose would need when they heard approaching hoof beats, and an authoritative call for Francis to come outside.

'That voice sounds familiar,' Francis said with displeasure. 'I believe that Sheriff Sutton has arrived.'

He went outside, where the sound of a brief conversation could be heard by everyone around the breakfast table. Then Francis re-entered with a tall, florid-faced man in tow.

'I'm not sure if you've met my wife and sister-in-law,' Francis said casually as he waved in the general direction of the table. 'The two men are Bailiff Mountsorrel from the town, and one of his constables, Robert Bishop. This is Sheriff Sutton, everybody.'

'I know Mountsorrel, certainly,' Sutton confirmed, 'and his presence here is fortuitous, since perhaps he can explain if his own sheriff, Anthony Gamble, has recently experienced a loss of his wits.'

'Not to my knowledge, sir,' said Edward, 'although for a while he seemed to be of the belief that he could countermand instructions that came directly from Westminster.'

'That may explain things, perhaps,' Sutton said with a frown. 'I first of all received an instruction from the attorney general's office, to the effect that Barton here was to be relieved of normal duties while he went in search of traitors. Then I was sent a note from Gamble that I was to ignore the attorney general's command, and finally — only yesterday evening — I got a dispatch from the attorney general confirming his original command and instructing me to ignore anything I might have received from Gamble. There was also something about a curse, and I am instructed to ensure that this notice is copied and nailed up for public view in every alehouse, church porch and crossroads in the county. That's primarily why I'm here, Barton, since that will be your allotted task for the next few days.'

Francis suppressed a groan, and Edward asked, 'Do you say that I am now to obey the first order I received from London, sir? And if so, is Sheriff Gamble likely to have received the same countermand to his order that you did?'

'No idea,' Sutton replied curtly, 'but you may take it from me that you are to proceed as first instructed by London. If Gamble raises any objection, refer him to me.'

'Do you and he enjoy a particularly close relationship, sir?' Francis asked disingenuously.

'Far from it,' said Sutton with a look of distaste. 'Your employer, Mountsorrel, is a pompous oaf who believes that being the most successful wine importer in the town gives him additional status, quite apart from his success in wheedling a sheriffdom out of those who owed him money at the time. If you want a true account of the character of Sheriff Gamble, enquire of Sheriff Freeman. And now I must take my leave, if I am to meet with the lord lieutenant of the county for dinner at his home in Calverton.'

After Sutton left, they finished loading the last of the items onto the wagon and Kitty bid Rose a tearful farewell, while Edward and Francis reminded Robbie that Rose was in his sole care for the foreseeable future. The loaded wagon with its two passengers rumbled down the lane towards the track that led to Arnold, and from there north-west towards Bestwood and Blidworth. Rose and Robbie looked back for one final wave, and Francis turned to Edward.

'Well, I know what I'll be doing for the next few days,' he said. 'At least we may be assured that the curse will be sufficiently well broadcast by the time Rose takes up her temporary new residence. What had *you* in mind?'

'I shall take up Sheriff Sutton's invitation to learn more about Sheriff Gamble from Sheriff Freeman,' said Edward. 'The two are not on the friendliest of terms, and I may learn something that will aid our search for those who planned the downfall of His Majesty.'

11

'I hardly see the need for you to consult with me, given that you seem to take all your instruction from Sheriff Gamble,' Sheriff Freeman observed coldly as Edward sat in the chair opposite his before the blazing fire in the drawing room of his mansion in Bellar Gate.

'That is because it is always Sheriff Gamble who gives me instruction, whether I am seeking it or not,' Edward explained tactfully. 'That is largely why I sought this audience, in the hope that you might clarify my precise position regarding certain orders that I received from London, by the hand of one Walter Emerson. I was in the process of carrying out those orders when Sheriff Gamble instructed me to ignore them and desist from further enquiry into the matters in question. He was then apparently overruled by London.'

Freeman sneered. 'That was typical of that fool Gamble. My apologies — please ignore that. I must own that I find his approach to the office that we share to be as inconsistent as his business practices.'

'You obviously have the advantage of me there,' Edward admitted, hoping that this would not be the end of the revelations. He was not disappointed, as Freeman sat back in his padded chair, sipped a little more wine and continued.

'Sheriff Gamble and I are connected in matters other than our joint duties as sheriff. He is, as you are no doubt aware, an importer and seller of wines and other liquors. Until recently he appeared to have a comfortable monopoly on such trade within the town, due largely to his ability to charge the lowest prices. I, as you will also be aware, sell cheeses and smoked goods, and as prominent local traders we are both afforded respected positions in the local Tradesmen's Guild. It is through that connection that I am aware that for some unaccountable reason, Gamble recently raised his prices to almost double his former rates, thereby losing all but a few of his regular customers and tottering on the brink of financial ruin. Then, for reasons that are equally inexplicable, he reduced his prices to their former level, and now prospers once again. So, as you can see, he is as inconsistent in business as he is in the discharge of his shrieval duties.'

'But you can confirm that I am once again free to pursue those matters entrusted to me by the emissary from London?'

'I can, but I would appreciate it if you could tell me what they might be.'

Edward thought hard for a moment, then concluded that it would be as well to keep on the right side of the man who could keep Sheriff Gamble off his back, and opted to tell at least some of the truth. 'You will recall that almost two weeks ago there was a dreadful fire in a row of houses in Halifax Lane that resulted in four deaths? Well, the people who died were Thomas and Agnes Whitely and their daughter Catherine, and a man from out of town who was temporarily renting the house next door to theirs, where I believe the fire originated.'

'Yes indeed, a terrible business, and the sooner the town authorities pass bylaws to prevent houses being constructed so closely together, the better. It's not as if there's a shortage of suitable land in the town. But what of this fire?'

'There is every reason to believe that it was caused by an explosion, and that the source of that explosion was gunpowder that was being stored in the house next door to Whitely's — the one rented by a man who we now know was named Solomon Calvert. My enquiries thus far have revealed that the explosion may have come about by accident, when this man Calvert and his landlord Whitely were arguing over the possession of a set of keys. I believe that a pistol was drawn and fired, almost certainly by Calvert, who was determined to retain those keys.'

'For what purpose?'

'Therein lies the root of the mystery,' said Edward with a frown. 'The keys in question gave access to a low alehouse called The Pilgrim, which lies at the foot of the castle rock, and is therefore strictly speaking within the jurisdiction of the county. I therefore called upon Bailiff Barton to assist me, and between us we determined that anyone armed with those keys could gain access to the castle itself by means of a corridor towards the rear of the alehouse. It connects with a passageway cut into the rock itself that snakes its way up into the castle proper. We believe that Calvert was planning on using this passage to introduce gunpowder into the castle.'

'Surely the castle garrison have enough gunpowder of their own?' said Freeman.

'Indeed that is the case, but my masters in London believed that the gunpowder being stored in Halifax Lane was intended for use in an attack on the castle by the same group of conspirators who recently failed in their attempt to blow up His Majesty during the opening of Parliament.'

'They have surely all been captured and thrown into the Tower?'

'I have already disclosed more than I should have,' Edward admitted, 'but you should know that it is the belief in London that the planned death of the king was merely the prelude to something with much wider implications.'

'I am the Sheriff of Nottingham, and you are my bailiff!' Freeman retorted, bristling. 'Or at least, I'm one of those to whom you're answerable. It ill behoves you to claim that there are matters that you should not be disclosing to me! Now, out with the rest!'

'My profuse apologies,' Edward muttered, 'but the need for utmost secrecy makes me both cautious and forgetful. The truth is that the planned explosion in Westminster Hall was intended to be the beginning of a total overthrow of power within the realm, and the installation of a new monarch who might be more favourable to Catholics.'

'Must all those who were once deluded into following the old religion be held suspect?' Freeman complained. 'If so, then you must add me to your list, since it was the religion in which I was raised. It was only the wisdom and merciful grace of Her late Majesty that taught me the error of my ways. Surely, there must be more behind it than the matter of how one worships God?'

'There still remain those whose adherence to the old religion drives their actions, even at the risk of their own lives being forfeit,' Edward told him. 'But I am advised that they have recruited others whose only motivation is material gain, and the desire to create havoc in the running of the nation. It is those that I have been commissioned to identify and seize. The "lesser mortals", if you will — those who are now seeking to hide, obscuring their own involvement until someone else calls them back into action.'

'You believe that they may be found here in the town?'

'Also in the county,' Edward added. 'One of the leading conspirators in what they are now calling the "Gunpowder Plot" was a man called Robert Keyes, who had his family home in a place called Staveley, across the border in Derbyshire. I have discovered that he has family connections with a dissolute group living in the Skegby area, and I am in the process of investigating their recent activities. I believe that I am on the right track, because there have been attempts to deter both myself and Bailiff Barton from making further enquiries in their direction.'

'When you came here enquiring about Sheriff Gamble's attempts to call off your investigations,' Freeman began hesitantly, 'were you perhaps of the belief that he too might be one of those involved locally in this broader plot?'

'It had occurred to me,' Edward admitted, 'although only with the greatest misgivings. But since we are at this point in our confidences, who do you know to be those with whom he regularly associates?'

'There's a local moneyman called Aaron Drucker, whose primary business used to be as a general merchant, selling items such as farm tools, crockery, ironmongery and the like. But he branched out into more luxury goods, and soon had a need for a secure vault in which to place his more valuable items, along with his personal wealth. This in turn led him into the loaning of sums to other tradesmen by way of temporary "accommodation" for short-term requirements. It is popularly believed among the members of the Tradesmen's Guild that Gamble had resort to him during the time in which his trading income was declining, and he needed to replenish his stock. Other than that, Gamble's only associates are those like myself, men of substance in the town — merchants, farriers, fullers and suchlike.'

'Where does Drucker have his place of business?' Edward asked.

'On Timber Hill, convenient for the weekly market. His is the triple jettied house that overlooks the Malt Cross. Are you minded to pay him a visit?'

'In due course,' said Edward. 'First I must learn more about the possible reasons for Sheriff Gamble's fluctuations in trade, and for that I need to renew my contact with London.'

When he arrived at Ashby, Edward immediately made his way to the Porters' cottage and found his wife sitting beside her mother's bed.

'She's sinking more each day,' Elizabeth wept as she buried her face in Edward's tunic sleeve. 'I can hardly bear to remain by her side when she calls out in pain, and pleads with God to ease her suffering. Should I come to this one day, please just run me through with your sword.'

'Does she take anything to eat or drink?' Edward asked.

'A little mulled wine, but I fear that we have little of that left to give her.'

'I will obtain more,' Edward promised, as he reached inside his tunic and extracted a carefully sealed bag. 'Whenever you serve her wine in future, place several of these grains in it prior to the heating of the liquid. It is a simple supplied by Rose, and she assures me that it will relieve her suffering.'

'It will not deprive her of what little life she has left?' Elizabeth asked, conscience- stricken.

'Rose assures me that it will not. But should she be proved wrong, her life may be hard to bear anyway, if it is so beset with pain.'

'She is not the only one who suffers,' Elizabeth replied with a nod towards the open door. 'You no doubt saw Father sitting outside when you first came in?'

'I did,' Edward confirmed.

Elizabeth's lip trembled. 'He's been there for two days. He can't bring himself to come inside, and he won't eat. I fear for him when Mother is no more. Please go and speak to him, Edward.'

Edwin Porter gave no sign of acknowledgement when Edward sat beside him on the long bench by the front door. To break the silence, Edward gazed up at the clouds stacking up in the west behind the lowering sun and observed, 'You'll get very wet if you stay out here all night, to judge by those clouds.'

The only response was a grunt, and Edward tried again.

'I was just thinking back to my childhood in that orphanage in Leicester. I'd have given anything to have parents and grandparents.'

'At least you didn't have to mourn the passing of someone you loved deeply,' the old man muttered bitterly, but this only made Edward more determined.

'And why should my children have to mourn the passing of *two*?'

'I'm not dead yet, more's the pity.'

'But you will be if you sit out here in the rain for too long,' Edward countered. 'Then who's going to pass on your wonderful skill for carving children's toys out of wood? I'm sure that Robert would love to learn, and you can't deny Margaret the chance to take over the cooking when her grandmother's gone, can you?'

'I'm not hungry.'

'But you will be eventually, and even if *you* aren't, right now I could eat a horse. Provided that there was a suitable sauce to go with it, of course.'

Edwin couldn't suppress an instinctive chuckle, and this somehow unblocked the emotional fountain that he'd been suppressing for some time. Tears began to roll down his ruddy cheeks, and Edward placed a comforting arm around his shoulders.

'Come on, old man,' he murmured, 'time to rejoin the family inside who are missing you.'

Later that night, Elizabeth clung to Edward in the old barn next door. She'd been sleeping here ever since her arrival, leaving her dying mother the comfort of the cottage's only bedchamber.

'How did you manage to make my father talk?' Elizabeth asked him.

'I just asked myself how I'd feel in his place,' Edward replied. 'I take it that you'll be staying on after ... well, after ... you know?'

'Of course,' Elizabeth confirmed, 'but don't forget where to find us, and come back regularly.'

'I will,' he promised, 'but I shall have to leave you briefly after speaking with the earl tomorrow. I'll be back within a week, with more of Rose's simples.'

'They probably won't be needed by then,' Elizabeth croaked. '*Please* don't go away and leave me to deal with Mother's passing alone. *Please*, Edward!'

'I promise I'll stay,' he assured her as he snuggled his head into hers. 'But there will come a time when I will have to return to the town, you know that, don't you?'

'Of course — just don't go yet.'

'I was very sorry to learn of your wife's mother's illness,' Earl Henry Hastings told Edward quietly over wine and wafers the following morning. 'She was highly regarded as the housekeeper here in her day, while her man was the perfect steward. I shall make the necessary arrangements for her to be buried here on the estate.'

'That's most gracious of you,' Edward replied as he bowed his head in acknowledgement. 'It is unlikely to be much longer. But of course that is not why I sought this early audience.'

'I assume that you have something of import to pass on to London?'

'Yes, in one sense, but no in another. In truth, I need further enquiries to be made into the background of the sheriff whose order you were required to countermand — Sheriff Gamble. It would seem that for some time he enjoyed the ability to charge the lowest prices for his wine imports, thereby all but closing down the competition from others. Then he appeared to suffer a lapse in that advantage, only to have it restored shortly after that fire that killed Calvert. I strongly suspect that the two events are linked.'

The earl thought for a moment, then nodded. 'I believe that your suspicions could be well founded. You may recall that during our last meeting, I told you of Calvert's background as a merchant who travelled the whole of Europe, and was therefore well placed to make contact with those who meant no good towards England. Well, one chosen intrigue that was identified was termed "commercial starvation", and it took the form of undermining the nation's revenues by blocking trade outlets, banning imports of English goods into foreign ports, and — most significantly in terms of what you suspect — the evasion of import taxes on goods. You are familiar with Exchequer procedures?'

'Not really,' Edward admitted.

'Since the days of the seventh Henry, who inherited a bankrupted throne,' the earl advised him, 'one form of income for the nation's Treasury has been a tax on the import of certain goods,' Hasting explained. 'Luxury goods in the main, but wine has certainly been subject to such levies for at least the past one hundred years. It is currently set at such a rate that the merchants who import foreign wines have no recourse but to add that sum to the price that they charge for their product.'

'And if for some reason they are exempt from such a levy, then their goods are correspondingly cheaper?' Edward suggested.

'Precisely. But very few are exempt from such taxes, and in the main those that are will be found to be royal favourites, or those who have given some great service to the nation. There is no reason to believe that Sheriff Gamble falls into either of those categories. If we are correct in the supposition that he has been importing wine without paying the import tax — or "tunnage" as it is termed in relation to wine — then this would explain his ability to undercut the prices of rival merchants.'

'But how might this be achieved?'

'The masters of most of our ports — and certainly the major ones — are obliged to keep scrupulous records of cargoes being unloaded. Some of the more trusted ones are also obliged to collect the tunnage due from the master of the vessel, or its owner, before the cargo may be unloaded, but in all cases a record is sent to the Exchequer in London. However, it is well known, but little broadcast, that there are means of avoiding such an imposition.'

'Dishonest harbour masters?' Edward guessed.

'Certainly, and if caught they are subjected to terrible punishments, of which a heavy fine is arguably the most merciful. But there are also certain ports that are not blessed with officials at all — places where there are wharfs in which cargoes may be disembarked without any official note of their arrival. To mention a mere handful, there is Lymington in Hampshire, Fowey in Cornwall and Sutton Bridge on the coast of Lincolnshire. This information must be kept strictly between us, of course.'

'Of course. But if the existence of such ports is known, why has the illicit import of goods not been suppressed?'

'It is, but only to a limited extent,' Hastings replied with a frown. 'For every illicit cargo of which we are advised, there are believed to be a handful that pass through, disguised as other goods, or wrongly ascribed in the bills of lading and other shipping documents. A man like Calvert could easily have made arrangements for wine to be slipped into the country and delivered to Gamble without payment of tunnage, either in exchange for favours or a small bribe.'

'Little wonder that Gamble was seeking to throw me off the scent, if he was party to such an arrangement with Calvert!' Edward said. 'And no wonder he hired someone to take a pistol shot at me, when he learned that we'd been tasked with investigating the plot to seize the castle. We have him!'

'No, we do not,' Hastings cautioned. 'For one thing, we have yet to ascertain that it was Gamble who ordered the attack on you, and whether or not he's been evading tunnage in the manner imagined. In order to prove the latter, I shall require you to provide me with an inventory of recent additions to Gamble's stock-in-trade, with particular reference to where it originated — France, Portugal or wherever. Even then we need to establish the nature of the "favour" required of him by Calvert in return for access to tax evasion. But did you not tell me that Gamble has recently been able to reduce his prices, even though Calvert is dead? How can this be?'

'I have the answer to that,' Edward said. 'Gamble is known to be very friendly with another importer of goods into the town, a man named Aaron Drucker. This man Drucker may either have inherited the business of Calvert, or it may simply be the case that he has been running such a scheme himself for some years, and that Gamble dealt with him rather than Calvert. If that is the case, then I fear that my further enquiries may lead nowhere.'

'But they must still be carried out, and without delay,' Hastings insisted.

'I fear that there *will* be some delay,' Edward replied sadly. 'I shall first be required to attend a family funeral.'

Rose waved as she saw Robbie wandering up from the surrounding trees with yet another armful of substantial tree branches, which he dropped on the pile to the side, then picked up his axe.

'Is it really going to be rabbit stew for dinner?' he asked.

She chuckled. 'Since it was rabbits that you caught, what else? Catch me a young deer and you can have venison pie tomorrow.'

They both looked down the grass slope as the sound of approaching hooves became audible. A large, unkempt man rode into sight, sitting in a cracked saddle on a tired-looking nag. He dismounted and strode aggressively towards Rose, then stopped when he saw Robbie approaching from his right, carrying a large axe.

'Who are you, and what are you doing in this cottage?' the man demanded.

Rose looked down her nose at him as she replied, 'My name is Rose Middleham, and I've taken up residence here, along with my son.'

'Says you!' the man replied with an ugly sneer. 'My name's Jamie Saunders, and this cottage belongs to me!'

'Then I know who to thank for his generosity in granting a wise-woman somewhere to lay her head,' Rose replied, seemingly undaunted.

'A wise-woman, eh?' Saunders challenged her. 'So you could cure my warts, that right?'

'I could if you had any,' Rose replied calmly as she looked more closely at him. 'And I could give you something for that dose of the pox you picked up a few months ago from that prostitute in Skegby.'

'I'll be back,' Saunders announced as his face went pale, and he stepped back a few paces. 'Then we'll talk about how you can pay your rent.'

As his horse disappeared back down the slope, Robbie watched, open-mouthed.

'Does he *really* have the pox?' he asked.

Rose nodded. 'But I could probably have guessed that anyway. Why, did you doubt my powers?'

When Robbie shook his head, Rose chuckled.

'Then you'd better get on with chopping that firewood, before I turn you into a toad.'

12

On a day in early spring, the Mountsorrel and Porter family stood with their heads bowed, partly out of respect for the departed soul who was being laid to rest, and partly to avoid the harsh rays of sunlight high in the sky. The local clergyman had been summoned by the Earl of Huntingdon, and was reciting the Church of England liturgy for the burial of the dead over the recently dug hole in the ground. Catherine Porter's simple grave would soon be marked by the rudimentary cross carved by her grieving widower from cypress wood, which according to ancient folklore had the power to ward off evil spirits. The old ways might have been banned from Church rituals, but statute would never eliminate rural traditions and beliefs.

The mourners were a silent group in a silent location — the ground to the side of Ashby Castle in which generations of the Hastings family were interred, with ornate crosses and headstones marking their final resting places. If they were conscious of the honour that was being bestowed upon the former estate housekeeper, those she had left behind showed no sign of it in their solemn faces. Edwin Porter was making no sound, but tears were running off the end of his chin onto the fancy ruff that his granddaughter Margaret had made for him from some old lace. Margaret held one of his hands now, while her brother Robert held the other, and it was their simple but loving gesture that was preventing the proud old man from howling out his grief. The other two grandchildren, Joanna and Edwin, clung to their mother's skirts, looking to her for guidance as to how one was supposed to behave during this unfamiliar ceremony.

Elizabeth clung to Edward, her head buried in his shoulder as her shoulders heaved with misery. In many ways the passing of Catherine Porter had been a blessing, a merciful release through the grace of God, but one could not endure the loss of a mother without shedding copious tears.

As the houseboy from the castle threw the last of the earth over the body six feet below, encased in a heavy shroud, the family turned and walked sadly back to the cottage.

'You kept your promise,' Elizabeth said to Edward as she handed him a mug of their remaining wine, 'and I would not seek to take advantage by asking you to tarry here any longer. For one thing, it will be a house beset by sadness for many weeks to come, and for another you have your duties to perform.'

'My first duty is to my family, as you have often reminded me,' said Edward as he took the mug and kissed her forehead. 'I can remain for a few more days at least, if only to ensure that your father does not do away with himself.'

Elizabeth shuddered, then took the mug from Edward's hand before wrapping herself around him and allowing the tears to fall yet again. 'God bless you, Edward,' she croaked. 'I know that I sometimes chide you when I feel that your duties come before your family, but these past few weeks have shown me another Edward Mountsorrel — the one I fell in love with.'

'None of that!' came the disapproving voice of Margaret, as she entered the main room and saw her parents entwined in a comforting embrace. 'I need Father to help Grandpapa bring in some of the wood that he and Robert have cut for the fire. Then I need Mother to help set the board while I see to the roast that's almost ready for serving.'

Edward and Elizabeth exchanged loving glances as Edward said, 'Let's hope that your father takes as much comfort in our children as we do, since they may be his path out of despair.'

'There are days when they are *mine*, too,' Elizabeth replied. 'Thank you for giving them to me.'

Two weeks after Catherine's funeral, Elizabeth was assuring Edward that his continued presence was no longer essential, and Edwin was clearly feeling guilty, believing that Edward had only remained in Ashby for his sake.

'I'm not going to do away with myself, lad,' Edwin assured him late one afternoon as they sat outside with mugs of beer, 'so you can safely go back to your duties. Nottingham must be turning into a right unruly place without its bailiff, so off you go in the morning.'

Edward duly complied, lingering only to hug the children, kiss Elizabeth tenderly on the lips, and shake Edwin's hand. He then trotted his mount onto the path that led north towards the Wilden Ferry, on the other side of which he turned to the east and entered the town by way of the former abbey at Lenton, sadly falling victim to both nature and the vandals who'd stripped out most of the stonework.

The house in Whitefriars Lane felt cold and abandoned as Edward unlocked the front door and stepped inside. He looked sadly towards the grate, expecting to see ashes that needed to be cleared away before he could light a new fire to ward off the chill, and was both surprised and delighted to see that the task had been completed for him. As if in acknowledgement of his immediate thought, the scullery door opened, and in came Meg.

'So you're finally back,' she said, beaming. 'I've been back a day or two, and I was beginning to wonder if something had happened to you. Were you in Ashby all that time?'

'I'm afraid so,' Edward confirmed. 'The mistress's mother died, and I had to remain for a little while to look after things. But I'm back now — is there anything in the larder?'

'Not until I get to the market, but I'm sure the pie sellers are still in the streets, so you'll have to make do with that. But I'll give you some pork for your supper, if that's what you'd like.'

'Excellent,' said Edward, 'but you're not back in residence, are you? Only I wouldn't want people spreading ill-founded rumours, with just the two of us here. I'm only thinking of your reputation.'

'I've already got one!' Meg chortled. 'According to my sister, you and me have been at it for years, whenever the mistress is away.'

'We can't have that!' Edward protested. 'You'll need to return to your sister's house in the evenings.'

'No bloody chance of that! Those kids of hers are likely to turn me grey afore my time, and I'd rather be thought of as a loose woman than suffer another night with them.'

'We'll talk about this again this evening,' Edward insisted, 'but in the meantime I need to get back to work. If you could put some fresh, dry linen on the bed, light a fire and leave some cold pork for my supper, that would be more than sufficient.'

An hour later, as Edward appeared in the front doorway of the Guildhall, there was a faint cheer from the constable on duty at the front desk.

'Thank God you're finally back!' he said. 'The senior constable's been like a dog with a sore behind for weeks now, and he's starting to give orders like *he's* the bailiff.'

'Ask him to come down to my room without delay,' Edward instructed as he descended the rear stairs, armed with two steaming mutton pies wrapped in a handkerchief. He was just finishing the second of them, seated behind his desk, when Senior Constable Durward appeared in his doorway.

'Welcome back, sir,' he said. 'And not afore time, if I might make so bold.'

'You may,' Edward replied, 'but go and get yourself a seat and tell me what I've been missing.'

Durward dragged the bench into the room from outside. 'There have been heaps of burglaries and God alone knows how many alehouse brawls, and the prostitutes are back to parading on the north side of the marketplace on Saturdays. It didn't help that you sent Robbie Bishop away again.'

'He's engaged on important work in the county which has a bearing on recent events here in the town,' Edward assured him, 'but that reminds me — what can you tell me about a man called Aaron Drucker?'

'The moneylender up on Timber Hill?' Durward asked.

'The very same, although I believe that he's also a general merchant.'

'Oh aye,' said Durward. 'A seller of other folks' property, anyroad.'

'Your meaning?'

'Well, it's like this, sir. Drucker has this safe vault in his basement, see, and folks come to him to have their valuable possessions kept nice and secure. Only those who do business with him get their houses broken into not long after, and I reckon that they only get marked out once Drucker knows who's got something valuable and who hasn't.'

'If I understand what you're telling me,' Edward began, 'Drucker gets to know who the wealthy people are in the town when they call on him to have their valuables kept in his secure vault, then those same people have their houses broken into shortly afterwards.'

'Yeah — it doesn't pay to let Drucker know that you've got something worth stealing.'

'But surely, if you have your suspicions, you must have taken steps to investigate?'

'Of course we have,' Durward replied, 'but then we get told to back off, and we're threatened with the law if we push too hard in our enquiries.'

'Who orders you to back off?' Edward demanded. 'It's me you take your orders from, remember — why haven't you reported any of this to me in the past?'

'You were away, sir — every time. The first couple of times you were up in Daybrook with the other bailiff, and the last time was when you went down to Ashby. We were reporting directly to the two sheriffs while you were away, and it was Sheriff Gamble who said to leave things as they were.'

'And what did Sheriff Freeman have to say?'

'We didn't think it necessary to ask him, sir, since we'd got orders from the other sheriff. That was all in order, wasn't it?'

'I suppose so, but what sort of legal threat did Sheriff Gamble hold over your heads in order to persuade you to leave well alone?'

'Well, it wasn't so much a legal threat as a reminder that if we disobeyed the orders of a sheriff, we could all be out of a job.'

Edward considered all this for a moment, then nodded. 'You acted appropriately, Jack. Leave it with me. Do you by any chance know who might have carried out these burglaries on the information supplied by Drucker?'

'Not really, sir, but he's got a nasty collection of bruisers who hang around his premises all the time, and there are one or two of them who've got a history when it comes to breaking into other folks' houses. There's Joby Tinker, for a start.'

'Yes, that would make sense.' Edward remembered that Joby Tinker was only one more conviction away from a hanging, and this planted the seed of an idea in his head. It would be a hazardous venture, but something bold was called for. 'How many men can you make available late at night, all in the same place?'

Jack Durward thought for a moment. 'Six, probably, if I switch two from the Day Watch. But you'd be leaving the rest of the town unpatrolled, and the Good Lord alone knows what might happen if folks at the other end of town got to learn about it.'

'You'll just have to keep it quiet then, won't you?' Edward said. 'But I'm not saying that it'll be tonight, or even this week. I'll speak with you again before I need you to organise it. Now, perhaps you'd better get back to your normal duties.'

'I don't believe I've had the pleasure of making your acquaintance,' oozed the tall, overweight man with long, black locks. 'I'm told that you're the town bailiff, on whom we all rely for our safety. I sincerely hope that the occasion of this visit is not to tell me of a threat to my secure facilities?'

'Quite the contrary,' Edward replied with a forced smile. 'It is those very "secure facilities" that I wish to make use of. I'm reliably advised that Master Drucker has the finest available vault in Nottingham, and I have several items of great value that I wish to preserve.'

Drucker looked him up and down with an expression of disbelief. 'Without wishing to be impolite, or to cast the slightest aspersion on the word of a man of the law, I would not have imagined that a bailiff was so well remunerated as to have accumulated any great wealth.'

'Nor would I have done,' Edward assured him as he noted the avaricious glint in Drucker's eye, 'had it not been for the recent death of my wife's mother. She lived in retirement in Ashby, where the rest of my family are still residing, and since my duties regularly take me away from my house in Whitefriars Lane I'm anxious to ensure that it is not exposed to burglars while certain items are lodged in the side cabinet in my main room. They may not be of any great financial worth, but given their origin they have great sentimental value, and may indeed be regarded as collectable.'

'And what, pray, are they?'

'Items of personal adornment that the good lady had acquired over the years in which she was the housekeeper at Ashby. Such was the respect and regard in which she was held that from time to time her master would gift her with items that might be regarded as commonplace by him, but which a person of humble status such as she might regard as having some value in view of their origins.'

'Could you be more specific?' Drucker asked as he waved Edward into his client chair on the other side of his long desk, and rang the bell for an attendant to serve wine.

'Perhaps the most notable,' said Edward with mock pride, 'is a brooch on a gold chain. The brooch itself contains a miniature of the late queen, and was presented to a former Earl of Huntingdon for his service in raising an armed band against the threatened Spanish invasion. He was happy to part with it, given that the new king had recently gifted him with something similar. Then there is an amethyst ring that was once, or so it is rumoured, on the hand of the Countess of Nottingham. She was of course a lady in attendance on Queen Elizabeth while her husband commanded the English Fleet that sent the Armada packing. There are also several other items looted over the years from former abbeys upon their dissolution — altar sticks, chalices and the like. I believe them to have been worked in gold.'

'They would be of value, if only for their metal,' said Drucker, 'and you would do well to consign them to my safekeeping. My fee for such a service would depend upon my examining them for myself, you understand.'

'Of course,' Edward replied with a nod, 'but it will be some days before I can bring them to you, since I am required to travel north to Daybrook this evening, and to remain there for several days in company with my counterpart in the county. The house is currently empty, apart from a female servant who is only there by day, and so there is no-one else who might bring them to you for valuation.'

'Whenever is convenient to your good self,' said Drucker, 'but for the moment please enjoy the quality of this fine imported Burgundy.'

Thirty minutes later, Edward stepped back out into the bustle of Timber Hill with a feeling of great satisfaction. It was very generous of Drucker to toast his impending downfall with such a good wine. Now all that remained was for Edward to escort Meg back to her sister's house, whether she wanted to go or not.

Rose looked up from the pot in which she was stirring mint into a coney stew, and saw a somewhat elderly and pompous-looking man dismounting from a fine horse. She was aware of Robbie sidling in from her left, carrying more kindling to keep the open fire burning, and felt safe enough to hold the man's arrogant stare.

'So,' he began, 'the one they called "Magic Mary" has returned. Do you have more amulets to peddle to the gullible, or could you cure me of my gout?'

'I could if you so wish,' Rose replied calmly as she swiftly assessed the man, 'but you might prove more generous if I were to first restore your withering manhood.'

'So you still extort money for your simples?' the man asked, red-faced.

'I do. We each need to earn a living, and mine happens to be by means of curing ailments, predicting future fortunes and removing curses. You, I sense, were once an eminent person in a place that gave itself airs, and are now seeking some means of retrieving your lost dignity and boosting your self-importance.'

'Enough of your insolence!' the man bellowed, causing Robbie to take several steps in his direction.

Rose held up a hand to restrain him. 'Do not concern yourself over him, son — he's all wind and bluster, as he always was.'

'And who *was* I, then?' the man challenged her.

'The steward of Newstead, in the days when your master Sir John Byron was seeking to have me hanged as a witch,' she replied confidently. 'This came to nought when the truth came out during my trial in Nottingham, and I would imagine that yours was one of those behinds that were kicked by Sir John, who was never forgiving towards those who failed him. But you were never so important in my life that I can now recall your name.'

'Thomas Wilbert,' he reminded her. 'But if you were innocent of those allegations of witchcraft, why did you make yourself scarce?'

'I was *removed* from around here by a sheriff's bailiff, largely on the strength of false allegations made by yourself, when the only way you could induce your workmen to continue their repairs on your master's hall was to turn a blind eye to the amulets they bought from me to ward off the ghost of the Black Monk. I spent some time locked in a cell in the town, and while left to my own thoughts I heard a call of distress from someone I had believed was lost to me. *This* fine strapping young man, as it transpires. His name is Robert, and he's my son.'

'There was no talk of any son when you were living in Linby or Papplewick,' Wilbert replied suspiciously.

'Not every woman wishes to boast of having given birth to a bastard, and the man who sired him left me to fend for myself when he took the infant with him in his desertion, only to abandon him in an orphanage in Leicester. Many years later Robert was working for a pittance in an alehouse in Quorndon, pining for a mother he somehow knew he still had, and I was able to locate him using my special powers. Special powers that I suspect you have need of, since I do not think you took the trouble to ride for half a day from your current residence in Hucknall simply to discover the fate of an elderly wise-woman.'

'There is not much that escapes your knowledge, is there?' said Wilbert, the wind taken out of his sails.

'There is not,' Rose agreed, 'so how many friends do you wish to bring here?'

'You *know* the purpose of my visit?' he asked as his jaw dropped open.

'Its general nature, certainly,' she replied. 'You have all fallen victim to a curse that you wish to have removed, have you not?'

'We have,' he confirmed. 'Can you do that?'

'It will depend upon the nature of the curse, and whether or not you can pay my fee,' she replied guardedly. 'It is not as simple as removing warts, or curing the pox. I place myself in great danger when I step in front of a witch's curse.'

'But you are prepared to do it?'

'For the right fee, certainly,' said Rose. 'I shall require you all to assemble here on the day of the next full moon, and each of you must bring a cutting from the hairs around your private parts — along with my fee, of course. I shall also need to know all your names in order to enrol you in the lists of those exempted from the evil. And now, if you will excuse me, I have to attend to our dinner. I imagine that coney stew is not to your liking, so I bid you good day.'

'Do you *really* need them to cut hairs from round their privates?' Robbie asked as he watched Wilbert disappearing back down the slope towards the road.

'Of course not,' Rose replied with a grin, 'but even a witch is entitled to a little fun in her work.'

Edward lay wide awake and fully dressed on the bolster in the bedchamber of his house, a sword by his side and his ears primed for the slightest sound. He allowed his thoughts to drift to Elizabeth and the children, hoping that they might by now be sufficiently bored by the tedious routine of life in the Ashby house to be ready to come home.

Then he heard a telltale crack as a door somewhere in the house was forced open, probably with an iron crowbar. It was far enough away to be the door that gave access to the scullery from the rear garden. Edward's suspicion was confirmed when the same sound, but much louder, betrayed the similar fate of the inner door that gave access to the main room.

Once the stealthy footsteps had crossed the wooden floor, it was time for him to slip from the bed and execute the next part of his plan.

13

Edward leapt out into the main room with his sword raised to shoulder height, and there before him stood one of the largest men he'd seen for some time, armed with a massive iron crowbar. He raised it above his head as he rushed towards Edward, apparently undeterred by the sword. Edward jinked to one side in an attempt to thrust under the man's armpit, but was thrown off balance when he collided with the corner of the dining table to his left. The crowbar came down heavily at an angle to the base of his neck, and he fell to the floor, the sword clattering away to his right.

With a yelp of triumph his adversary grabbed the sword and pointed it downwards towards Edward's prone body, just as a massive club blow was delivered from behind to the side of the assailant's head. He was knocked off balance, and at least four arms appeared from behind him and grappled him to the floor.

Edward rose hastily, retrieved his blade, and pointed it at the man's throat. 'We'll begin with your name, shall we?'

The man stayed mute.

Senior Constable Durward told Edward, 'That's Joby Tinker, sir.'

'I though the smell was familiar,' Edward jested, then instructed his men to lift Tinker to his feet and hold him securely. 'What are you doing in my house?' he asked Tinker, who responded by launching a mouthful of spittle in his direction.

'He busted the back door, sir,' Constable Jenkins told him. 'We were lurking in that room by the kitchen in the garden when we saw him come over the garden fence.'

'I hope you didn't leave any mess in my housemaid's room,' Edward replied, then looked back at Tinker. 'You were sent here by Aaron Drucker, weren't you, to burgle my house?'

'I'm saying nothing,' Tinker insisted.

'That will suit me admirably just at the moment, because I intend to return to my bed while these good gentlemen escort you to the Guildhall,' said Edward. 'I'm aware of your history of burglaries and other offences, and I have no doubt that in the very near future I'll have the pleasure of leading the escort that takes you up the Mansfield road to the gallows at the top.'

'Says you,' Tinker retorted. 'I've got powerful friends, I have.'

'Let's see how influential they are while you're all sharing the same smelly room below the Guildhall,' said Edward. 'Take him away, gentlemen, while I catch up on some sleep.'

The following morning, Edward had Tinker dragged from his cell, unfed, unwashed and looking far less confident of his immediate future than he had the previous night. His hands and feet were bound tightly, and he was ordered to stand in front of Edward's desk, which he did with an expression of sullen resentment.

'No doubt you've had ample time to consider the depth of trouble that you've landed yourself in,' Edward gloated. 'To the charge of burglary I've added a charge of assaulting an officer of the law with intent to murder, so the hangman won't be entirely idle following the forthcoming Assize session.'

'What's it worth?' Tinker demanded.

'You think you can bribe me?' Edward asked. 'If I accepted every bribe that I'm offered by people like you, I wouldn't be eking out a living as a bailiff. I'd either be enjoying a rich life in a fancy townhouse, or long dead on the end of a rope for betraying my office.'

'I ain't got no money, anyroad,' Tinker admitted, 'but I know folks that do.'

'Like Master Drucker, you mean?'

'Not him, necessarily,' Tinker muttered. 'But men like him.'

'Of course, you wouldn't want to peach on Aaron Drucker, would you?' said Edward. 'Because he employs other pond scum like you, and one word against him from you would see you up a dark alley with your neck slit. Unless, of course, Master Drucker was himself in irons in the same unhealthy place where you spent last night, and many more nights to come before we load you into the wagon destined for Gallows Hill.'

'If I give you the stuff you need to lock him up, will you promise to do that, then let me out of here and give me a two-day start?' Tinker asked hopefully.

Edward pretended to be thinking the proposal over carefully. 'What can you possibly tell me about a fine upstanding gentleman like Master Drucker?' he asked eventually.

Tinker was only too happy to oblige with a torrent of words. 'He does special trips to the sea — well, he sends others like me to do them for him. There's lots of stuff coming into Nottingham that nobody's ever going to pay taxes on, and he makes a fortune out of selling them on. I can tell you some of the folks who buy them, and all, if you want to do a trade.'

'Tell me what sort of items you're talking about, and who buys them from Drucker,' Edward replied, 'and we'll talk seriously about your release.'

'Well, there's cloth and jewels, and sometimes statues and paintings,' said Tinker. 'But mainly it's wine in barrels — big bloody barrels that take three men to lift them.'

'And who exactly buys that from Drucker when it comes into town?'

'The sheriff, for one. That's why they haven't hung me yet. The last couple of times I got caught, the sheriff made sure there were no charges brought against me, and the time afore that he told the judge it couldn't have been me who was seen sneaking off down Fletcher Gate, because I'd been doing work for him in his orchard at the time.'

'Which sheriff was this?'

'I didn't know we had more than one. I'm talking about that little fat one with the wine business — Gamble, isn't that his name?'

'There is a Sheriff Gamble, certainly,' Edward confirmed. 'And you say that he buys wine from Aaron Drucker that's come into the country from somewhere on the coast without any taxes being paid?'

'Yeah, that's right.'

'Where on the coast?'

'Don't know exactly where, but it takes us a few days to get there with a line of wagons, and you go by way of Grantham. It's tricky near the end, because there are lots of marshes and quicksand.'

'You're almost a free man, Tinker, but one more question, and I want a totally honest answer. Have you ever been required to move barrels of gunpowder?'

Tinker nodded. 'I was hoping you weren't going to ask about that, because it'll mean that I'm in trouble for that house in Halifax Lane that got blown up.'

'And why should that have been your fault?'

'Well, it was me and another man who delivered it there, in the middle of the night, to a man I'd never seen afore. But he had a note from Drucker to say he was the one to deliver it to.'

'So you're telling me that you delivered gunpowder to a house in Halifax Lane on the orders of Aaron Drucker?'

'Yeah — two barrels. Full, they were — in fact, one was overflowing a bit, and some got spilt on the floor when we put the second barrel down. That's how I knew it was gunpowder, and the man we were delivering it to called us clumsy oafs. He said we could have got ourselves blown up. There were other barrels of the stuff there already.'

Edward remembered that Robbie Bishop and his father had also been paid to deliver barrels of gunpowder to Solomon Calvert's house. There must have been more than one shipment — no wonder the house had been completely destroyed. 'Anything else you can tell me about Aaron Drucker?' Edward asked hopefully.

Tinker shook his head. 'I've told you enough to get me killed as it is — unless you're going to let me go free. If you do, I can promise you that this town will never see my face again.'

'I think I can fairly say that you just talked yourself out of a noose, and a possible slit throat from your former employer,' Edward replied. 'And any arrangement that keeps your thieving hands out of Nottingham meets with my approval, so you'll be released after dark this evening, and don't let our paths cross again.'

After celebrating with two mutton pies from the vendor at Weekday Cross, Edward strolled down Bridlesmith Gate to the workshop of the town's most skilled and successful carpenter, Henry Bassett. He arranged for Bassett to call at his house later that day and mend two shattered doorframes, replacing the original locks with new ones for which Edward pocketed the keys. Then he left word with Jack Durward that he was journeying back to Ashby for several days, and that the town would again be relying on its senior constable.

The next morning he left one of the new keys with Meg at her sister's house, telling her that he hoped to be back in under a week. He then climbed into the saddle and nudged his horse's head westwards, in the direction of the ferry that would take him south over the county border into Leicestershire.

'Father's much improved,' Elizabeth told Edward as he dismounted outside her father's cottage. She wrapped her arms around him and felt him wince. 'Are you hurt?' she asked with a look of concern.

'I was, but it's only bruising now,' he assured her. 'Still, you have to be careful when grabbing me like that.'

'It's perhaps as well that you've decided to return to the safety of Ashby,' she said, frowning. 'Have you come to take us back home?'

'Can your father be left?'

'Probably — particularly since a lovely lady from the village came to pay her respects when she heard of Mother's death. She's a widow herself, and she brought him a lovely pheasant pie. She's promised to look in on him every day, so who knows?'

'It sounds as if you might acquire a stepmother,' said Edward.

Elizabeth tutted. 'Only you could think like that. Anyway, come inside and have some dinner. But be warned — Margaret has delusions that she can cook.'

As soon as they saw Edward, the children raced across the kitchen to greet him.

'Don't jump all over your father!' Elizabeth warned. 'He managed to get himself hurt in a fight that he'll probably try to deny if I probe further, but no doubt he'll be departing shortly for the castle up the drive, to explain to someone more important than me how he came by those injuries.'

'I need to speak to the earl, certainly,' Edward confirmed.

'I baked coney pasties for dinner,' Margaret chimed in, 'and you can't possibly leave without tasting at least one of them.'

'Very well,' said Edward. 'I've already hazarded my life once in the past few days, and I survived that, so let's have dinner, shall we?'

Two hours later, the Earl of Huntingdon smiled at the news that Edward had brought him.

'Excellent progress, Edward, and it ties in very neatly with advice that I received only yesterday from London, namely that your Sheriff Gamble paid no import taxes on any wine for as long as the records went back. I think we may safely conclude that at the very least he's been looking the other way while dark deeds were being committed within the town. He may even have been complicit in a conspiracy to load gunpowder into the castle.'

'This must surely mean that he'll be dismissed from office?' Edward suggested.

The earl shook his head. 'That won't be necessary, for at least two reasons. The first is that we don't wish to alert any others who may be implicated that we're aware of what's been going on. The second is that his term of office is due to expire at the end of this month anyway. His replacement, Robert Parker, has already been selected, so I suggest that we simply allow Gamble to complete his final two weeks in office, then have him arrested along with any others you manage to identify as being complicit in this outrageous plot to commandeer Nottingham Castle. How far have your enquiries progressed in the county?'

141

'I've arranged for Rose Middleham, sister-in-law to Bailiff Barton and a respected wise-woman, to pretend to lift the curse on all those involved in the plot. As part of that process, she'll claim to require their names, and by this means we'll have a list of the conspirators, supplied by themselves. When we next speak, I hope to be able to tell you that my plan has yielded rewards. And now, if I might be excused, I have some family business to complete.'

'I can see no reason why you can't take us back with you,' Elizabeth complained when Edward announced his intention of travelling back north alone. 'Father is restored to good spirits, and we may even be in his way now that he's enjoying the visits from Widow Catchpole. Or did you manage to set the house on fire, and are too afraid to tell me?'

'Nothing like that,' Edward said with a chuckle. 'It's just that — well, for a little while persons of a bad disposition may attempt to thwart my plans to unmask them, and I don't want to have to worry about you and the children perhaps being used as hostages to my actions.'

'You're telling me that you've become a target for a collection of brutes, and you expect me to remain here and worry that I'll never see you again?'

'I was thinking more of the children,' Edward explained. 'The same group that we're seeking to identify and hunt down took young Richard hostage, although he was able to escape. I don't want to take the same risk with our four, that's all. And you, of course.'

'Thank you for including me on that list,' Elizabeth replied sarcastically, then slipped gingerly into his arms as her face softened. 'Will there ever come a time when you seek some other office, so that I won't spend half my life worrying about becoming a widow?'

'I don't know any other way of life,' Edward admitted.

'But there comes a time when everyone has to adjust to change, surely? Father's had to adjust to losing Mother, I've had to adjust to being a mother of four, and Francis no doubt had to adjust his life considerably when he married Kitty. I take it that he's also involved in whatever you've got yourself into?'

'He is,' Edward confirmed, 'but I think he'd rather just be growing apples.'

Elizabeth kissed him on the lips. 'Off you go, you mad adventurer, and do your best to stay alive. Someone has to encourage Margaret in her cooking, and you were very brave in eating two of those oversalted coney pasties.'

'Let's hope that's the worst hazard I'll have to confront in the immediate future,' Edward replied as he turned and headed through the front door.

Rose Middleham took a deep breath and prepared herself for what would be the greatest performance of her life. She'd never been one to fake her second sight or pretend to possess powers that she didn't have, mainly because she felt sure that if she resorted to trickery, like so many others of her former calling, she'd be deprived of that wonderful gift of being able to see into people's lives and diagnose their ailments. Now she had to make a big show of delving into the black caverns of necromancy, and she could only hope that the good spirits who had guarded her in the past would stand by her, given that she was doing this for the best of reasons.

There were over twenty people assembled on the lawn immediately in front of the cottage that she'd temporarily taken over. Robbie had been meticulous in collecting their coins, their pubic hair, and all their names on a long sheet of parchment. Given his illiteracy, he'd had to ask each of them to sign, and it was to be hoped that the names that had been supplied were genuine. In order to ensure that they were, Rose had been at great pains to explain to those who'd gathered that the 'special powers' she was about to invoke could only be summoned once, and would only be for the benefit of those who had actually paid for the privilege, and were named in her invocation.

Robbie slipped her the list, and she stepped forward and threw some special powder — saltpetre laced with copper beech resin — onto the flame in the chalice a few feet in front of her. As the bestial smell that came from the animal dung from which the saltpetre had been composed began to drift in the early afternoon breeze, she launched into her theatrics.

'Lord of the Pits of Hell, regard this, the obeisance of your handmaiden Rose Middleham, and grant her humble request that these here named by her be forever freed from the wicked curse of she who has sought to ensnare their souls in perpetuity. May they be forever cleansed of her pestilential attendance upon them, and may they walk in the protection of he who is Lord of all Misrule, and the generous guardian and benefactor of those who shower him with reverence. So be it decreed, and so be it executed. Praise be to thee, oh Master of the Dark Places and Ruler of Hades.'

She lifted the list of names into her line of vision, and read each of them solemnly out loud. Then she began to shake and sank to the ground in a seeming fit. This was Robbie's cue to rush to her side and pretend to rouse her from her coma, waving with one hand as he called out to the assembled company, 'Stay back, good sirs! My mother's been briefly taken over while the spell she's weaved lifts the curse from you all. Give thanks for her powers, but keep well back, I pray you.'

'Don't waste any time, don't lose your way, and don't get distracted,' Rose urged Robbie as she bustled him out of the cottage door later that day, handing him a cold ham slice and two pieces of her mint loaf for the two-hour ride. 'This list must be handed to Bailiff Barton as soon as he wakes in the morning. Tell him that I'll remain here to act as his guide when he brings the men in to seize the ones on that list.'

Robbie trotted the old carthorse up the grassy slope and onto the track that led back to Ravenshead, and from there down through Arnold back into Daybrook. The old nag seemed to be enjoying having a man on its back rather than shafts down its flanks, and went along happily as Robbie hummed a tune and imagined the warm welcome back in Daybrook.

As he rode through a dense patch of overhanging trees an hour or so away from his destination, a man armed with a pistol stepped out onto the track and ordered him to halt. Believing that he was about to become a victim of a highway robber, Robbie pulled on the reins and was about to announce that he was a constable engaged in his duties when he received a blow to the back of his head that was so forceful that it knocked him from the saddle and onto the dusty track. A fusillade of kicks to the torso and head ceased hurting when he lost consciousness, and the man with the pistol urged his comrades to search Robbie's clothing. Satisfied that they now had the tell-tale list, they rode off chuckling, leaving Robbie for dead.

An hour later, Rose was roused from a deep slumber by heavy and persistent knocking on her cottage door. She wandered out sleepily to answer it, and came wide awake when the barrel of a pistol was stuck an inch away from the end of her nose.

'Right, you witch,' said a gruff voice, 'you're finally going to get the hanging you deserve.'

14

Robbie came round deep into the night, aching in every conceivable bone, and with a pounding in his head that impaired his vision and balance. The horse had been grazing patiently nearby, and his first two attempts to remount proved ill-advised as he fell back into the dust. Then he resigned himself to jumping full length across the beast's shoulders and smacking its flanks in a sign to move on.

The beast obviously knew its way home, and when Francis slipped sleepily out of the house on his morning visit to the lean-to jakes to one side of the cottage, he came abruptly awake to the sight of the horse munching contentedly on the grassy approach to the orchard, with Robbie seemingly asleep across the animal's neck. He raced over and shook Robbie sharply by one arm, causing him to slide off the horse and crumple in a heap on the ground after letting out a loud groan of pain. Then his eyes opened and he asked, 'Am I back in Daybrook?'

'Where did you expect to be?' Francis asked. 'At least the horse knew its way home. What in God's name happened to you, and where's Rose?'

Robbie took a frustrating moment to gather his memories together, then looked back up at Francis with horror. 'I got waylaid on my way back. Two of them, at least, and they kicked and punched me.'

'What about Rose?' Francis all but screamed. 'Is she still alive?'

'I don't know,' Robbie admitted. 'She was when I left her, back at the cottage. But that was last night — or was it the night afore?'

'Why were you attacked?' Francis demanded. 'Did your ruse not fool anyone?'

'It seemed to,' Robbie replied, 'but they must have seen through it, else they wouldn't have done that to me, would they?'

'If they saw through it, and gave you a beating, God knows what they're likely to have done to Rose!' Francis wailed.

Kitty appeared in the open doorway in her floor-length nightgown and demanded, 'What was that about Rose? And why's Robbie lying on the ground? Has something happened to them both?'

'Robbie can't even seem to remember why he's back here,' said Francis.

Robbie scrambled to his feet, then recalled, 'I came back here to bring you the list.'

'What list?' Francis demanded.

Robbie reached inside his jerkin, then pulled a face. 'It's gone,' he admitted. 'They must have taken it.'

'Taken *what*?' Francis asked.

Robbie's face fell. 'A list of the names of all the folk that came to get their curse lifted. Rose gave it to me to bring to you.'

'So you were robbed of the list, and you've no idea what's happened to Rose? Is that all you can tell me?' Francis demanded angrily. When Robbie nodded sheepishly, Francis turned on his heel and stomped angrily back into the house.

Kitty looked across at Robbie with a face full of anguish. 'Is it possible that my sister's been murdered?'

Robbie nodded, then lowered his head. 'I don't know what went wrong, or what's happened to her, but it wasn't my fault, honest!' he mumbled through his tears.

Kitty turned and followed Francis back into the house, where he was in the process of buckling on a sword belt. 'Are you going out to look for Rose?' she asked.

'I am,' Francis replied. 'Whether she's alive or dead, I've got to find out, and that halfwit clearly can't help, so it's down to me.'

'That "halfwit", as you call him, is seriously hurt, and it's hardly his fault if he got set upon.'

Francis shook his head. 'Perhaps, if I can find Rose, she may remember some of the names on the list.'

Kitty stepped back, her eyes blazing with anger. 'If she's still *alive*, you mean! Is that all you can think of — that she may have something to tell you regarding the business that may have cost her her life? She's my *sister*, remember! My lovely, caring, kind, sweet…'

The rest of what she might have added was lost in a howl of grief, and Francis stepped forward, intending to take her into his arms, but she pushed him away angrily.

'Find her, Francis!' she said miserably. 'Bring her back alive, or, God help me, I'll never again regard you as a husband of mine for as long as we live. Never, do you understand?'

Back outside, Richard had fetched a cloth and dipped it in the water butt, and was doing his best to wipe mud and blood from Robbie's face and arms. Little Amy was sitting on an upturned wheelbarrow, quietly watching the proceedings. Robbie was just considering whether or not he might ask for a mug of water when Francis came striding out purposefully from the house and pierced him with a glare.

149

'The horse you arrived here on has been fed and watered during your absence. Even if you don't know quite where you are, or even what day it is, do you think that your beast could get you back into town?'

'Of course,' Robbie growled, 'and I might even get more respect from it than from certain folk around here. Why are you asking?'

'Because someone needs to ride back into town and report your failures to Bailiff Mountsorrel. Ask him to get up here without delay, and to bring some *real* constables with him.'

'Leaving here will be a pleasure,' Robbie announced with a snarl. 'I suppose you're about to have your breakfast?'

'No,' Francis replied coldly. 'Thanks to you I have to leave without delay and round up my constables from Arnold, Bestwood and Hucknall before I make some attempt to rescue Rose — assuming that she's still alive. Tell Bailiff Mountsorrel to meet me at the cottage where she was staying.'

The fact that Rose was still alive owed much to her inventive mind, and her contempt for the intelligence of the oafs who were threatening to hang her from the rope that they'd strung up outside. It was swinging lazily in the mid-morning breeze from the lintel above the front door of the cottage, one of the few timbers that appeared to be intact.

But, being the lackwits that they were, her captors had failed to get on with what should have been a priority in their evil agenda, and had instead become fixated on their own bodily needs. There was a large pot of coney stew left over from a batch that Rose had prepared the previous day, and it sat over the ashes of the spent fire. It had been spotted by the man who now appeared to be their leader, and who the others referred to as Master Ralph. He was one of those who had sought relief from the imaginary curse, and had given the name Ralph Keyes. Whoever he might be, he was clearly respected by the band of ruffians who accompanied him, which included, so far as Rose could recall, Thomas Wilbert, the former steward of Newstead, and Jamie Saunders, along with three others. That made six men to capture and hang one middle-aged woman, which gave her some idea of just how effective and well organised this local shambles of a gang were. When Ralph Keyes sniffed inquisitively at the pot and enquired what was in it, Rose saw her chance, and set about playing the part of a terrified old lady.

'If it please you, master, it's some coney stew that I was about to serve for my son's breakfast. I don't know where he's got to, but if you're prepared to let me live a little longer, I'll heat it up for you all to enjoy. I'll even make you some bread to go with it.'

'We know where your so-called "son" is,' Keyes sneered, 'and we've taken steps to ensure that he got no further than Bestwood. So he won't be needing it, will he?'

'If it will delay the moment when you hang me, would you like me to warm it up for *you*?' Rose asked desperately. 'There's probably enough for you all, and I can add a few rare spices to make it even more acceptable for gentlemen of quality such as yourselves.'

'Don't you enjoy your work more when you get them so scared of dying that they'll do anything to please you?' Keyes asked as he turned to address the others.

'I'm certainly hungry,' Wilbert growled, 'and we don't need to be back in Skegby until nightfall. She's going to swing sooner or later, so let's do it on a full stomach, I say.'

Rose controlled her breathing as the men untied the ropes around her wrists and allowed her back inside the cottage.

151

They mounted a guard on the only door, leaving the rest of them to sprawl lazily on the grass slope in front of the cottage, in happy anticipation of a good feed.

Once inside, Rose reached eagerly into her herb box for a generous handful of mandrake root, which she chopped finely, then mixed with some rosemary. She scurried back outside and rekindled the fire, then when it reached a suitable heat she stirred her deadly mixture into the stew with her iron ladle. Under the pretence of needing to re-enter the cottage for the required number of bowls and spoons, she hastily scanned the ceiling for any sign of the hole that Richard had said he had made in it, prior to climbing up into the roof to escape his captors. Then, as quietly as she could, Rose moved the old table to a point immediately under it, ensuring that there was a chair conveniently close to it for when her plan came to fruition. Satisfied, she hurried back out with oatmeal, salt, water and a mixing bowl and began stirring it all together. Ralph Keyes looked up lazily and challenged her.

'What are you doing now, you old sow?'

'Making some bread, like I promised,' Rose replied as innocently as she could.

Keyes pushed himself to his feet and walked over to look suspiciously into the mixing bowl. 'How do we know you're not planning to poison us?'

'I promise you I'm not,' Rose replied. 'If you like, I'll take some of the mixture myself,' she offered, praying that Keyes wouldn't insist that she do the same with the stew. When he agreed to her offer, she dipped the spoon into the bread mix, doled out a generous portion, then screwed up her face as the cold, slimy concoction slipped down her throat. Then as a distraction she told Keyes that there would be a delay while the bread making process was completed, but that the stew might now be warm enough to eat.

'Let's see then, shall we?' Keyes replied, and picked up one of the three wooden bowls that Rose had laid to the side of the pot. With an ingratiating smile, Rose filled the bowl with lukewarm coney stew, and when Keyes nodded his appreciation, she offered the remaining two bowls to Wilbert and Saunders, apologising for the fact that she had no more bowls, so they would have to take it in turns. There were several angry exchanges as the men fought to acquire a bowl, and Rose allowed herself a secret sigh of relief that they had all eaten at approximately the same time. It was vital that they all be overcome at once, before those who had been obliged to wait before eating saw the effect that the stew had on the others.

The quantity of mandrake root that Rose had stirred into the pot would, if consumed by one man, be instantly fatal, but if consumed in the diluted form that her captors had received, she hoped it would at least send them all to sleep. It might cause the more susceptible of them to hallucinate, but she could deal with that if it arose. The only outcome that her plan required was that they sink back senseless on the grass for a few minutes.

The first to succumb were those who had eaten either first, or more greedily, and Rose concealed her satisfaction as she saw Keyes lie back on the grass.

'Just going to get a few minutes of shut-eye,' he said feebly. 'Wake me up when it's time for the hanging.'

He was followed, one by one, by each of his comrades, one of whom called out, 'Martha? What are you doing here? You're supposed to be dead,' before sinking back in a coma. Relieved that no-one had thought to tie her hands again once she'd offered to feed them, Rose stepped silently back into the cottage, placed the chair on the table, climbed onto it, then before it could wobble too much reached upright until she could feel the ceiling beam. With a silent prayer, she heaved herself into the roof space and out of sight, suppressing a cry of disgust as she disturbed a family of rats on her way in.

Two hours later the men who had planned to hang her came round one by one, sitting upright, shaking their heads, then rising groggily to their feet. Keyes was one of the last to rise, and when he saw the others staggering around like alehouse drunks he blasphemed, then said, 'The old sow must have poisoned us! She must have escaped while we were overcome!'

'Shall we search the house?' Saunders offered.

Keyes nodded. 'Yes, for all the use that will be. We've got until sunset to find her, so let's set about it. If we have to report to our masters that we've lost her, we'll be as dead as she's supposed to have been!'

From behind her peephole in the roof, Rose watched them riding off, then pondered how on earth she was going to get down from her hiding place. Those who'd searched the house for long enough to report that she wasn't to be found had taken their rage out on the furniture, which was no longer strategically placed to allow her to get down out of the roof without risking a long jump and two broken legs. For the time being, it would have to be just her and the rats.

Edward took one look at the battered and bruised Robbie as he staggered into the house in Whitefriars Lane, and called out for Meg to go and fetch a local physician who lived just around the corner. He then sat Robbie down and got him to explain all that had happened. Once he realised the enormity of the danger that Rose was in, he handed Meg a handful of coins and told her that when the physician had tended to Robbie's injuries, she was to arrange for the nearest local carrier to transport Robbie home, with instructions to his wife Mary that he was to remain in his own house until called for again by Edward.

His next task was to ride hard down to the Guildhall and collect as many men from the Day Watch as could reasonably be spared — which, in the event, proved to be three — then lead them on a madcap ride north.

It was late afternoon before the Nottingham contingent caught up with their county counterparts, led by Francis and looking mournfully down the slope towards the cottage with the rope hanging from its front lintel. Edward eased his mount into position alongside Francis's and asked quietly, 'Did they make use of that rope?'

Francis shook his head. 'No idea, since from this distance there's no sign of anyone. They hopefully took her somewhere else. We may still have a chance to catch up with them before … before…'

'Has anyone searched the house yet?' Edward went on quickly.

'We don't know if there's anyone in there, or if they're armed,' Francis replied. 'You and I are the only ones with swords, and what use are clubs against the weapons *they're* likely to have?'

'Then we'd better be the first in there,' Edward suggested, puzzled and a little concerned by Francis's seemingly defeated attitude — or perhaps he feared finding Rose's body inside. Either way, there was nothing to be gained by sitting silently in the lane, hidden by overhanging trees, so Edward dismounted and instructed his constables to follow him cautiously down the grassy slope towards the silent cottage. Francis appeared to snap out of his gloomy reverie and gave the same instruction to his men, and as the six constables armed with clubs fanned out and began to creep up on the cottage, Edward and Francis strode purposefully ahead of them, then leaped through the open door with their swords at waist height, poised to thrust unquestioningly at whoever sought to oppose them.

When they discovered the place to be empty, Francis gave a loud groan. 'Unless they buried Rose somewhere in the ground out there, they must have taken her off. Please God we can find her before any ill befalls her.'

'If you want to find me, look above your thick head!' came a familiar voice from the ceiling.

Francis gave a shout of joy as he saw Rose's face through the gap in the rafters. 'Rose, is it really you?' he called out.

'No, it's my resentful ghost, haunting you as punishment for the length of time you took to get here. Is Robbie safe? One of the men who captured me led me to believe that they'd done away with him.'

'He's still alive, and as witless as ever,' Francis replied. 'But the useless oaf lost the list you gave him of all those who came to have the curse lifted. I was hoping that you could remember some of their names.'

'I'll do better than that, if you place some furniture under here, so that I can climb down,' Rose replied. 'And stop being so impolite about poor Robbie. He's a lovely boy. Did they hurt him badly?'

'One of them broke his wrist when he punched him in the head,' Francis jested as he gestured for Edward to pull the table under the hole in the rafters. 'See if you can land on this,' he called up to Rose, 'and if you fall, Edward and I are well placed to catch you.'

Rose leapt down in a flurry of skirts, then leaned on the shoulder that Edward made available in order to get down from the table. 'At least one of you knows how to be gallant to a lady,' she said as she hoisted up her outer skirt and fiddled in a pocket sewn into her kirtle, from which she removed a length of parchment. 'I took the precaution of making a copy of the list that Robbie was bringing you, in case he was waylaid. Call it second sight if you wish, although I prefer to think of it as the product of finely honed wits.'

Edward read the list and gave a low whistle as he looked across at Francis. 'If these names are correct, then we've stirred up the biggest wasps' nest that this county has ever seen. All we have to do now is summon up royal troops and find out where they're all skulking.'

'They said that they had to be back in Skegby by nightfall,' Rose told them, 'and it seems that those they called their "masters" will be waiting for them there.'

'Then we have no time to lose!' Edward said as he remounted his horse and turned his head south.

'Where are you heading?' Francis demanded. 'If it's Skegby, wait for me.'

'I'll leave Skegby to you for the moment,' Edward replied. 'Lose no time in finding out where the ones we're seeking are skulking, while I go and request royal troops.'

'You're planning on riding to London?' Francis asked in disbelief.

Edward shook his head as he dug his heels into his horse's flanks. 'Not London — Ashby. Keep things warm until we meet again in Skegby.'

It was pitch dark as Edward forced an exhausted Oliver down the final mile, towards the Porter cottage, as a church clock somewhere chimed the eleventh hour. He had no time to call in, indeed no time to even announce his presence, and he carried on as fast as the horse could carry him until he reached the main doors of the castle and hammered on them for admission. After what seemed like an hour, a sleepy-looking steward opened the door, then groaned when he recognised the late-night visitor.

'The master has just retired to bed!' he protested as Edward pushed past him and headed for the hall.

'Then get him up again, and find me some wine and something to eat — I have ridden hard with some vital intelligence to pass on to your master.'

The Earl of Huntingdon appeared a few minutes later, a riding cloak draped over his nightshirt. He frowned as he saw Edward tearing a cold roast chicken apart with grubby fingers, a mug of red wine in his other hand.

'I see that we are entertaining you well enough,' he observed with heavy sarcasm. 'My steward tells me that it's more than just a matter of filling your empty stomach.'

'Indeed it is,' Edward confirmed as he swallowed his latest mouthful. 'We have a list of those who are to be arrested for their plot to seize Nottingham Castle, and I require troops from the Tower to assist in their arrest and transportation south to London.'

'These things require a few days,' the earl cautioned him. 'I can arrange for a messenger to be sent to Whitehall without delay — probably before dawn — but you will need to rely on the castle guard being called out in the meantime. I'll have an order sent to Nottingham immediately. Will your quarry still be in your sights by then?'

Edward nodded. 'A contingent of local constables are heading to their hiding place, to the north of the county — a place called Skegby — and the county bailiff's been left in charge in the meantime. If we act quickly, we have them!'

The earl rang a bell on the small table to the side of where he'd taken a seat, and when the steward reappeared with sullen resentment written all over his face, he was given his instructions. 'Send Master Draper to Whitehall with a note that I shall have ready in a few moments,' said the earl. 'He is to place it in the hands of a Master Walter Emerson, and none other. There will also be a note to take to Nottingham, calling out the castle guard there, but Simon can be trusted with that first thing in the morning. The sooner you organise that, the sooner you may retire to your bed. I shall be in my private chamber with the necessary notes within the hour.'

The steward bowed out with a face like a long-dead lamprey, and the earl turned back to Edward.

'I thank you for your devoted service, Master Mountsorrel. The least I can do is allow you to finish your repast in peace. I shall give instruction that a bedchamber be made available for you, and ensure that the best attention is given to your horse. Now, if you would excuse me, I have matters to attend to, as you just heard.'

Edward thanked him and returned to ripping apart the remains of the chicken while drenching his parched throat with a fine wine. Then, as the effect of the food and wine began to blend with natural exhaustion, his eyes began to feel heavy, and he decided to rest his head on the board for a few moments before enquiring after the bedchamber he'd been promised.

He woke up with a stiff neck and a sour taste in his mouth just as the first light of the new day was appearing through the high mullioned windows of the hall. As his mind began to clear, he considered his options. He would need to return to Nottingham in order to await the men at arms from the castle that the earl had promised him, and somehow he had to make arrangements for someone to lead the Tower contingent to Skegby in due course. None of this allowed him the luxury of lying on a feather bolster as a guest of the earl, so he made his way wearily outside, relieved himself against the stable wall, then collected Oliver from the groom.

'He's a fine horse, sir, and seemingly none the worse for his long journey yesterday,' said the groom. 'He ate well, and drank two buckets of water. I took the liberty of rubbing him down, if that were in order, sir?'

Thanking the lad profusely, and handing him more coins than he probably earned in a month, Edward climbed into the saddle and trotted Oliver down the drive, intending to sneak past his own family in the cottage by the lodge gates. To his amazement and concern, as he rounded the bend that gave him his first sight of the cottage, he saw Elizabeth and the children seated in the family wagon. Edwin Porter was standing by the cottage door, obviously waiting to wave them farewell.

Edward nudged Oliver up to the wagon, and stared blankly into Elizabeth's smiling face.

'Did you *really* expect to get away with returning to town without us?' she asked, as she moved over on the front board, waiting for Edward to hitch his horse between the shafts.

15

'How did you know I was here?' Edward asked as he turned back from their final wave to his father-in-law and flicked the reins to indicate for the horse to turn right, and head north for home.

'You could call it a family conspiracy,' Elizabeth replied. 'Father was sitting outside, unable to sleep as usual, and enjoying the woodland night noises while wrapped in several blankets, when he saw you make a hasty dash up to the castle. We hadn't been told to expect you, and he feared that something might be amiss, so he woke me, and we decided to wake the children. Apart from little Edwin, of course, who makes up for the sleep that his grandfather seems to do without these days.'

'But how did you know that I wasn't intending to call in for breakfast?' Edward asked, still recovering from the surprise, and a little ashamed that his plan to slip furtively past his own family had been exposed.

'Once I expressed some doubt about whether you were back here for our benefit, or simply putting your duties first as usual, Margaret asked permission to go up to the castle and enquire regarding your horse. It seems that she got talking with the stable groom up there — whose name is Pip, by the way — and shamelessly wheedled out of him that he'd been instructed to have your mount prepared for a hasty departure at daybreak, and that messengers had been sent to London to have soldiers meet you in Nottingham without delay.

'We have at least two hours for you to tell your story,' Elizabeth continued, 'so, why has it proved necessary for you to spend more time with the Earl of Huntingdon than your family whenever we've been in Ashby?'

'The earl is in direct contact with those in London from whom Francis and I have recently received instruction.'

'But I thought that you reported, in the first instance, to your sheriffs.'

'Indeed we do, ordinarily,' Edward agreed, 'but this matter is far graver, and concerns the entire nation, not just Nottingham.'

'This is not the first time that you've been given secret orders from London, is it?' said Elizabeth. 'Just when Edwin and Amy were born, two years ago now, you and Francis took yourselves off down south in search of traitors. There was also that time before that, when you were briefly reunited with your mother, and we were obliged to take refuge in a church loft. Surely, by now, the two of you must have put paid to any rebels who resent our king?'

'You heard of the attempt to blow up Parliament, last November, with the king and half the nobles of the realm inside the chamber?'

'Of course, but I also heard that those responsible had been captured and locked away in the Tower of London. Are you about to tell me that there are some who remain unaccounted for, and that some of them may be found in Nottingham?'

'That's precisely the case,' Edward confirmed, 'and we're about to corner them and hand them over to join their companions in the Tower.'

'By "we", you mean yourself and Francis?'

'Yes, and also Rose, who was fundamental to our plan to flush them out into the open.'

'And how does poor Kitty feel about having both her husband and her sister dragged into what is essentially your mission?'

'It's not simply mine, since most of those we've identified are skulking away in the county.'

'Is it connected with that awful fire in Halifax Lane as well?'

'It is indeed. We believe that the real cause of the fire was an accident involving several barrels of gunpowder that were being stored in one of the houses. The plan was, or so we believe, to load that gunpowder into the castle, using a secret door at the back of The Pilgrim alehouse at the foot of the castle rock.'

'To blow up the castle, you mean?'

'Not necessarily,' Edward replied. 'It's more likely that it would have been an attempt to seize the castle, as part of a wider plot to take over the nation and install a puppet queen.'

'What's going to be happening next, and is there the remotest chance that we'll have you home with us for more than a few hours once we get there?'

'That will depend,' Edward replied guardedly. 'There will be troops coming north from the Tower in order to arrest those who Francis hopefully has surrounded in Skegby, and in the meantime I'll be riding north to join him with a contingent from the castle.'

'Real soldiers — at *our* house?' Robert asked excitedly.

'Yes, for a few minutes only, I suspect, until I ride north with them,' Edward replied. 'When you're likely to see me again is anyone's guess. Right now, get ready to cross the Trent on the ferry, and *don't* let Joanna dangle her hands in the water.'

The six constables had taken up positions behind the tall yew hedge that fronted the substantial but somewhat rundown farmhouse that sat out on the Tibshelf track, west of Skegby and almost on the Derbyshire border. This, according to Constable Tomlin, whose Hucknall territory included Skegby, was the former home of the Whitely family, and the only dwelling in the area large enough to hide the twenty or so fugitives from justice identified on Rose's list.

Rose was among those keeping careful watch from behind the hedge, although the list was now in Francis's possession as he stood alongside her. She'd already identified Wilbert, Saunders and Keyes, who wandered to the front windows from time to time. Francis kept looking anxiously behind him and down the track that led from Skegby, impatient for the sight of armed men on horseback who could surround the old farmhouse and flush out those inside.

But, as he reminded himself, he might not be the only one seeking reinforcements. He periodically urged the constables under his command to keep low in the ditch in which they were standing, while the only horse — Francis's mount Sally — was tied up in the trees on the far side of the track, safely hidden from sight. His caution was rewarded shortly after the sun rose to its highest point, and the sound of approaching hooves alerted the watchers to the arrival of reinforcements for one side or the other.

They had ducked down below the edge of the ditch just in time as three men on horseback appeared from the direction of Skegby. One of them was clearly the leader — a broadly built man of some substance, to judge by the quality of his riding cloak and plumed hat. 'That's bloody Drucker!' someone to the side of Francis whispered, and Francis hissed back for silence. Fortunately, the noise of three sets of horses' hooves on the hard dusty ground was enough to drown out this brief exchange, and the three new arrivals rode abreast through the opening left by the hanging gate that had been long in need of repair. They dismounted at the front door, and were welcomed and hastily ushered inside by the man previously identified by Rose as Ralph Keyes, then they were lost to sight.

'So who's that man you just recognised?' Francis demanded of Constable Giles, from Edward's Town Watch.

'Aaron Drucker,' Giles replied. 'He lives up Timber Hill with a fancy business, lending money to other folk and keeping their valuable goods safe in his basement. But the bugger's got lots of dodges on the side, and a few bruisers to do his dirty work. I recognised one of them riding alongside him — name of Jem Bolger, and a real nasty piece of work.'

'I've known worse,' Rose said. She looked at Francis. 'But that's just three more for us to keep an eye on while we await those soldiers that Edward promised us. Will they be coming all the way from London?'

'If they are,' Francis said with a grimace, 'then we're in for a long wait in this miserable ditch.'

They had no sooner unlocked the front door to their home in Whitefriars Lane, leaving Robert and Margaret to begin unloading the wagon, than Meg came running through the open door that led to the scullery.

'I'm *so* glad to see you all back home!' she called out.

Edward gave a hollow laugh. 'What she really means is that she's delighted not to have to spend another night at her sister's house, playing nursemaid to her children.'

'That as well,' Meg admitted. 'But I hope you're back for good, and you'll all be ready for some delicious meals.'

'Some of us will be,' Elizabeth said kindly with a sideways glance at Edward, 'but you're presumably familiar enough with the master's irregular attendances not to assume that he'll be home for any of those meals.'

'I'll certainly be home for the first,' Edward said, 'and I'm sure we're all hungry, so what can you offer us?'

'Nothing, at the moment,' Meg said with a frown. 'But the daily market down by the Guildhall should still be open, so what would you like, if I can get it?'

Edward and Elizabeth eagerly rattled off a list of items that they hoped might still be available from the traders' stalls, and Edward pressed some coins into Meg's hand as he bid her lose no time in seeking out what they wanted. He undertook to light the fire, while Elizabeth went in search of fresh bed linen, ordered the children to sweep the accumulated dust from the floors in each room, then set the table for supper.

By the time they'd all eaten their fill of the pickled pork, smoked ham, fish, fruit and manchet loaf that Meg had managed to acquire, night had fallen, and Meg sought leave to retire to her room in the garden.

'Before you go,' Edward asked, 'tell us what's been happening, who — if anyone — has called to see us, and what all the local gossip's about.'

Meg was eager to oblige, and Edward listened politely to her accounts of who'd been accused of infidelity with their neighbours, who had been hauled before the magistrates, how all the young girls seemed to be buying green cloth to turn into caps in time for the Spring Hiring Fair, and how the local butchers were conspiring to raise the prices of their joints of meat. Finally, she got round to concluding, 'Oh, and that Robbie Bishop come round here a few times, asking if you were back. It looked to me as if the injuries to his face were healing nicely.'

'*What* injuries to his face?' Elizabeth asked.

Edward explained how Robbie had been set upon and left for dead on his way back from Daybrook, but had been ordered home to rest and recover from his injuries until Edward called for him. 'By the sound of things, he's ready to resume duties, and I have a particular job for him.'

'The poor boy!' Elizabeth commiserated. 'I suppose that Mary's got used to having a man who comes home bearing the scars of his work — when he comes home at all, that is. I hope that whatever you've got in mind for him will enable him to spend at least some time at home.'

'Indeed it will,' said Edward, 'but it will be *this* home.'

The following morning, once the sun was sufficiently high in the sky to burn off the morning mists, Edward rode to Robbie's humble abode, where he was met by a smiling Mary Bishop.

'Thank the Good Lord,' she said. 'Now perhaps Robbie will stop mithering around the house like a dog that's been chained in its kennel. Have you come to take him back to work with you?'

'Only if he's fully recovered from his injuries, and is fit for duty,' Edward assured her. 'I'm sorry that I had to send him home to you in that state.'

'Serves him right,' Mary muttered unsympathetically, 'and at least he's finally learned that there are men bigger and tougher than he is.'

'There were three of them,' growled Robbie as he entered the house through the back door that led in from the small garden, 'and the sooner I can get my own back on them, the happier I'll be. But how's Rose — still alive, I hope?'

Edward looked at the scars on Robbie's face that might never fully heal, delighted to hear that his ordeal had not diminished his courage or enthusiasm for taking on wrongdoers. 'She is indeed, Robbie, so don't worry about her. I have further work for you, and it will be an indirect way of seeking revenge on those who waylaid you. They've retreated out Skegby way, and Francis is believed to be keeping a firm eye on their hideout, wherever it may be. I've sent for soldiers from the Tower of London, but they'll take at least a week to journey north. In the meantime, I'm being allocated a detachment of men at arms from the castle.'

'So what do you want me to do?'

'Wait here in Nottingham for the Tower soldiers, then guide them up to wherever I'll be with the castle troop. They'll no doubt be told to seek me out at my house, so you'll be based there to await them. At the same time, of course, you can once again guard my family.'

'But how will I know where to take the soldiers?' Robbie asked with a furrowed brow.

'I've no idea at present, but no doubt when they begin to approach Skegby, which is where you must take them, Francis or someone will become aware of their arrival and lead them to the right place. Let's get one task completed at a time, shall we?'

An hour later Elizabeth was welcoming Robbie back into her house, and ordering all the children to move their bedding out in front of the fireplace, so that Robbie could occupy the spare room to the side of the house that had become their bedroom over the years. He'd offered to sleep in the kitchen outside until Meg had objected, both on the grounds of hygiene and in order to preserve her reputation.

The following morning Robert, who'd been maintaining a vigil by the front door ever since their return, rushed into the all-purpose living room in which Meg was in the process of clearing the breakfast board, and said, 'The soldiers have come! The soldiers have come!'

Edward walked outside and looked up at the mounted troop of eight who were wearing the livery of a spreading green oak that identified them as being part of the castle garrison. At their head was a man in his late thirties wearing a gold helm that was crested to show that he was a man of rank, and as he dismounted he removed the helm to reveal a head of grizzled ginger hair that was greying in places. But his smile looked youthful enough as he held out his hand and introduced himself. 'I'm Captain Owen Makepeace, commander of the Nottingham castle guard. You, I assume, are the town bailiff?'

'That's me,' Edward confirmed as he shook the proffered hand. 'I'd invite you and you men to step inside and refresh yourselves, only…'

'Yes, quite,' Makepeace replied, almost disdainfully. 'There are too many of us to fit comfortably within your dwelling, are there not? No matter — our instructions are to proceed with you to wherever it is you require us to empty a nest of traitors.'

'Give me a moment, and I'll be back with you,' Edward replied, then disappeared back inside, ignoring eager questions from Robert and Margaret.

'How long *this* time?' Elizabeth demanded.

'No idea,' Edward mumbled as he hastily strapped on his sword and threw on his riding cloak. Then it was out to the stable at the side, where Oliver was already saddled. He rode him to the front of the house, where he fell modestly in place behind the second rank of armed horsemen and shouted to their captain that they should head out by way of the marketplace, then take the Hucknall track.

It was well past the middle of the day by the time that Edward called a halt outside the modest house in Sandy Lane in which he knew that Constable Tomlin normally resided. He may well have been taken on somewhere by Francis, but perhaps his wife might know where. It was the only hope he had of knowing where to lead the men, rather than be left looking like a clueless idiot.

Fortunately, Mary Tomlin knew more about her husband's movements than Elizabeth did Edward's, and in answer to his nervous enquiry she said, 'Jeb and that bailiff — you know, the good-looking one? — said they were headed for Skegby, and I heard something about the old Whitely house. You'll find that on the other side of Skegby, on the track to Tibshelf. If you sees Jeb, tell him that he's just become a granddad, on account of our daughter Lucy giving birth to a little girl during the night.'

Thanking her profusely for her assistance, and wishing her daughter and granddaughter the best of health, Edward allowed himself to be offered the lead position as the troop headed off westward. Just over two hours later, they heard a welcoming shout from a ditch to their left as Francis's face appeared above ground level. Then he looked uncertainly at the force that Edward had brought with him.

'They're just the advanced guard,' Edward assured him. 'There are others on their way from the Tower, but these should do for the time being. Which reminds me — which of you is Jeb Tomlin?'

'That's me,' Tomlin confirmed as his face appeared alongside Francis's.

'You became the proud grandfather of a baby girl earlier today,' Edward told him, 'and I suggest that you head back home without delay.'

'Don't you need me here anymore?' Tomlin asked hopefully.

Edward shook his head. 'No, but to you falls the important task of waiting in Hucknall until a contingent of armed men from the Tower of London arrive, led by one of my constables. When they do, direct them up here.'

'Surely we shouldn't be losing a man at this critical stage?' Makepeace argued.

Edward had other ideas. 'We'll be gaining far more if this man can direct the Tower guards in our direction. In the meantime, I imagine that we sit and wait.'

'Not in my orders,' Makepeace objected. 'My orders are to flush out traitors. Is that the house?' he asked Francis as he nodded towards the old farmhouse. Francis replied in the affirmative, then looked at Edward to smooth things over.

Edward took the point and turned to Makepeace. 'What do you suggest as our plan of attack?'

'Simple,' Makepeace replied. 'You and your constables move towards the house in plain view, armed with your cudgel things, and demand that the rebels surrender, on pain of having the thatch burned down over their heads. When they come out, we corral them into a circle, and your men secure them with the ropes that I hope you've come supplied with. I see that you have a woman in your party. She can stay well to the rear of all the action.'

'You've obviously never tried to give orders to my sister-in-law, who incidentally is a witch,' Francis said, only to be kicked on the ankle by an indignant Rose.

The plan of action was going well up until the point at which, on a shouted command from Edward, those who'd been lurking inside the farmhouse appeared on the steps that led down onto the grass in front of it. Then one of them — Drucker — raised his eyebrows in amazement and called out, 'Owen, is that *you*?'

'It is indeed,' Makepeace confirmed as he dismounted, ordered his men to do the same, then instructed that they draw their swords as he gave Edward a malevolent smirk.

'Thank you for your assistance in locating my colleagues, Bailiff Mountsorrel. Now you'll do me the courtesy of regarding yourself, and all your men, as my prisoners.'

16

'Did you *really* expect to break up a conspiracy that's been three years in the making, with just a collection of local bumpkins who call themselves "constables"?' Makepeace gloated as he looked down at Edward and Francis, seated on the hard wooden floor and roped together back-to-back, like everyone else in their party. They'd opted not to argue with men armed with swords, and were now being held in the main room of the former farmhouse, surrounded by those they had sought to bring to justice.

'May I assume that whoever it was in London who ordered you to give us assistance was also part of that conspiracy?' Edward asked.

Makepeace laughed. 'No. The idiot in London who requested armed assistance for your pathetic mission was unwise enough to go through the normal channels.'

'Ah,' Edward replied, as the reality sank in. 'Sheriff Gamble?'

'You're perhaps not as stupid as you appear,' Makepeace sneered. 'Not stupid — just far too impetuous. Look where it's got you *this* time.'

'At least I succeeded in identifying almost all of those in Nottingham and the surrounding countryside who were plotting to seize the castle,' Edward said glumly. 'Since you occupy a prominent position there, I assume that the plan wasn't simply to blow the place up?'

'Clearly not,' Makepeace confirmed. 'The gunpowder was never intended to be ignited. It was simply to be stored beneath the main armoury, with the threat of its use if the castle governor refused to yield it.'

'And none of that could be achieved without someone on the inside,' Edward concluded out loud. 'What was to be your reward?'

'The governorship,' said Makepeace with satisfaction. 'I've spent too long following the orders of others, and it was time that I ran my own operation. Regrettably, that will no longer be possible.'

'That's true for all of you,' Edward observed loudly as he cast his eyes round the surly crew who were standing guard over them, some armed with knives, two with swords, and the rest with an assortment of clubs. 'Now it's just a matter of securing your own survival, is it not?'

'Indeed,' Makepeace agreed, 'hence the importance of having something to bargain with when we demand a safe escape from here, preferably supplied with enough coin to get us across to the nearest amenable port of embarkation, and from there across the Channel.'

'I'll take a guess at Sutton Bridge,' said Edward as he nodded towards where Aaron Drucker was cleaning his fingernails with the tip of a wicked-looking knife.

Drucker raised his eyes and glared back at him, then across at Makepeace, as he responded with, 'I want the pleasure of killing *that* one.'

'But we'd be no use to you dead, would we?' Edward replied. 'We're only of use to you as hostages, isn't that correct?'

'Totally correct,' Makepeace agreed. 'Let's just hope that some fool is prepared to trade you miserable lot for some of the bravest men in England.'

'So brave that they planned to slaughter countless innocent men, women and children with a cowardly explosion simply because they existed,' Edward snarled, unable to restrain himself. This time, the response came from a man whose face

Francis remembered from the adjoining table in The Wheatsheaf in Skegby.

'They deserved it, the murdering bastards! They've tortured God knows how many innocent souls whose only fault was worshipping the proper way — the way we've been taught by Rome. I've got an uncle in prison in London, and every day they take him out of his cell and put the hot irons on him, or pull him apart on this here machine. Folk who do that don't deserve to die in their beds.'

'Presumably you haven't seen any of that with your own eyes?' Edward challenged him. 'You've been told that by others who were trying to talk you into doing *their* evil deeds, until you finished up no better than they are.'

'Shut your mouth, before I slit your neck from ear to ear!' Makepeace snarled.

Francis whispered in Edward's ear, 'We're in enough trouble already — don't provoke the man any further, for God's sake!'

But there was no stopping Edward now that he was in the middle of an argument that he thought he might win. Drucker was next to speak. 'What about all those they're torturing right now in The Tower?' he demanded.

'They're only seeking to extract information regarding who else was involved in the plot to remove King James from the throne,' Edward reminded him. 'The ones who could see nothing wrong with blowing up lords, bishops, royal children, the queen, and anyone else — like attendants and servers — who might get in the way.'

'That was a necessary part of a much wider bid for justice for those who wish only to worship in the way that God intended,' Ralph Keyes argued.

Edward laughed. 'Along with those who have no hope of advancement or wealth through their own efforts or natural abilities, but who seek to rise in society by stepping on others. Presumably you all met Solomon Calvert at some stage before his very fortunate death by his own stupidity? He wasn't even a Catholic, by my guess.'

'If you don't silence him, I will!' Drucker snapped as he moved alarmingly close to Edward, his foot raised as if to kick him in the head.

'Hold!' Makepeace commanded as he walked swiftly across the room and pushed Drucker away. 'Can't you see that he's simply trying to divide us, or divert our attention from our chosen strategy, which is to obtain our permanent freedom by holding them as hostages to our own release?'

'I was wondering what all that was about,' Francis muttered from behind Edward, as an argument broke out among their captors as to the best way of communicating their demands to those in authority.

'If you want to know what it was *really* about,' Edward replied as he twisted his head to be heard by Francis, 'perhaps you'd better ask your sister-in-law.'

Francis finally realised what Edward had been about when deliberately provoking an argument that could have got him killed. He looked round hastily, and his initial hope was confirmed. There was no sign of Rose, who'd presumably been overlooked in all the plotters' excitement at having captured hostages. Hopefully she was by now well down the road, seeking help. But who from? It was too much to hope that the soldiers from London were here already, and who was there locally who could come to their aid? There wasn't even a constable based in Skegby, although there should be. If Francis escaped this latest danger that Edward had got him into — or did he only have himself to blame? — then he'd take steps to ensure that there was.

As matters stood, perhaps they should be playing for time, since they could not even be certain that Makepeace and his private army were aware that men at arms were on their way from the Tower. This additional consideration almost certainly lay at the root of Edward's apparent stratagem of denying their captors time to think out their next move, or begin executions with a view to sending identifiable body parts to those who might be persuaded to bargain for the lives of the remaining hostages. It was time for Francis to make a contribution.

'I'm intrigued to know just who exactly you intend to make your demands known to,' he called out. 'This is the middle of nowhere, with no royal officials within a week's ride. Have you trained pigeons to fly down to London with your demands written on little pieces of parchment tied to their legs?'

'Would you like to die as painfully as your friend there?' Makepeace demanded with a nod towards Edward. He then turned to address his fellow captors. 'In case any of the rest of you were wondering the same thing, I despatched Ensign Winter back to Nottingham Castle less than an hour ago. He carries a note stating that unless safe passage is granted to myself and my followers, the hostages we have captured, including two upstanding local bailiffs, would have their throats slit and their carcases hung at a local crossroads, or from a convenient inn board. The governor of the castle has sufficient authority of his own to agree to such terms, and the garrison strongroom carries sufficient coin to fund our departure from this benighted country.'

'The country you were born in,' Edward put in, in a further effort to play for time, though he now realised that they had at least until the return of Makepeace's messenger. 'The land that will still be home to your wives and families, the land that is the only one in which your speech will be understood, the only one in which you may be gainfully employed…'

'That was your final warning!' Makepeace bellowed. 'One more attempt on your part to dissuade my colleagues from their true purpose and I'll open your poxy throat and let all the blood out!'

'Do as he says, Edward,' Francis called out, 'because the messages we left will have been read by now.'

Makepeace appeared to be as surprised by this disclosure as Edward was, and he could only hope that he could do justice to whatever ruse Francis had decided upon as Makepeace asked, '*What* messages?'

'You big-mouthed *idiot*!' Edward snarled at Francis, in an attempt to give the ploy credibility.

Makepeace walked across the room to stand over Francis with a drawn sword. 'I said *what* messages?'

'We left messages with various people, and in particular the local constable in Arnold, that if we hadn't returned by nightfall, word should be sent to Sheriff Sutton and Sheriff Freeman, and the local trained band should be mustered for our rescue. We already had our suspicions about Sheriff Gamble, you see.'

That provoked a hollow laugh from Makepeace. 'I'm the one responsible for the training of the trained band, and believe me when I tell you that they're no match for my men.'

'Obviously not, if you trained them,' Edward goaded him, receiving a kick in the ankles for his cheek.

'If it comes to killing off hostages as an incentive to the authorities, you'll be the first!' Makepeace growled.

The hostages were held in increasing discomfort for four more days, only being allowed outside for calls of nature, and they were given no food or drink, aside from tiny measures of small beer. Their captors, however, sent out at regular intervals for bread, cheese and ale from local alehouses.

There was no response from the castle to the ransom demands, and Edward was idly speculating over what the authorities might be planning when he was startled by a high-pitched shout from the front lawn.

'Release those you have in your keeping,' came the shrill challenge, 'or your souls shall rot in Hell!'

Wilbert strode to the window and looked out, then turned back to address those inside. 'It's that old bag who was pretending to be a witch!' he said, laughing. 'She obviously believes that we're still taken in by her pretences — I thought we'd dealt with her.'

'So did I!' Makepeace replied. 'She must have slipped away while we were busy rounding up the rest of this lot. I'll tell her to go away, and if that doesn't work, has anyone here got a bow?'

'There's one in the room to the back of here,' Saunders told him. 'It's a crossbow we used to kill crows that were after the wheat crop in the days when the family farmed this place.'

'Go and get it,' Makepeace commanded. Saunders slipped away through the door to the rear room, just as Rose recommenced her ranting.

'A curse on all those who hold as prisoners those who are dear to me! May lightning bolts strike them dead, and may their innards be consumed by rats summoned from the depths of Hades!'

'Go away, you old sow!' Makepeace said as he propped the crossbow on the window ledge and began to take aim.

'What does she think she's about?' Francis whispered in Edward's ear. 'She must realise that no-one's fooled by her anymore, and she'll just get herself killed!'

'She's not that foolish,' Edward counselled, 'and she must have a very good reason for her antics.'

That very good reason became obvious barely minutes later, when Francis and Edward turned in surprise as they felt their wrist restraints being untied. They were confronted by the grinning face of Robbie Bishop.

'Say nothing, but be ready to jump the soldiers,' he mumbled as he sat back with his hands behind him, posing as a prisoner himself.

'She's gone,' Makepeace informed the others as he stood back from the window.

Rose had created the necessary diversion for Robbie to slip into the house the back way, unnoticed while all the attention was being given to her ranting on the front lawn. Edward was just asking himself what was coming next when a loud voice boomed out a command from somewhere outside.

'This is Major Brindley, of the Yeomen Warders of His Majesty's Royal Palace and Fortress of the Tower of London. I have thirty men under my command, and you are surrounded. We know that you have prisoners, and unless they are released where we can clearly see them within the next minute, my orders are to enter your hiding place by force of arms, and if necessary kill you all. You are alleged traitors to the lawfully crowned king, and whether you die by our hand or take your chances at trial is a decision that you must now make.'

'Remain where you are!' Makepeace shouted to all those he commanded. 'We will get no fair trial, nor will they risk the lives of our hostages by moving in on us. The man is bluffing.'

'So what do you suggest that we do?' Drucker demanded.

'We kill our first hostage, and throw his corpse out there to prove that we mean business!' Makepeace said. 'The lives of those we have captured are obviously of some value to them, else they would not have sent Tower men to rescue them. Let's see how they respond when we lob the head of one of their bailiffs out onto the grass!'

'Time to move, sirs,' Robbie announced as he rose quickly to his impressive height.

Makepeace stepped in front of Edward, allowing both bailiffs the opportunity to scramble upright. Then Robbie took a few steps and loomed directly in front of the man with the crossbow.

'I'll make a better target than either of the men I work for. So let fly, then you'll have nothing left to shoot with, will you?'

'Where did this oaf come from, and why are all their hands untied?' Makepeace demanded in outrage as he briefly took his eyes off Robbie. Seeing his momentary distraction, Robbie dived at him, bringing him down with a massive thud as the crossbow flew out of his hands and skidded across the floor. Francis took his opportunity and raced after the weapon, hurriedly re-loaded the bolt and pointed it directly at Drucker.

'I believe that the odds have just changed in our favour,' he observed drily, 'so either you all proceed outside as ordered, or Nottingham will be one criminal less in number. And believe me, it would give me immense pleasure to perform that duty, so don't take any more time to consider your options.'

Edward hastily untied the remaining constables as their former captors shuffled outside, to the most impressive sight that Skegby had ever seen. The property was completely surrounded by armed men in royal livery, each holding the bridle of his horse with one hand, and brandishing a shiny sword at waist height with the other. Their commanding officer stepped forward and called out, 'Bailiff Mountsorrel, please identify yourself.'

Edward did as requested, and stepped out onto the grass. 'You made good time from London,' he told Major Brindley, 'but not a moment too soon. I can supply the names of all those who are to be arrested and taken down to London. They are led by this man behind me — "Makepeace". He's a disgrace to the livery he bears, but as you can see he is — or perhaps I should now say, *was* — the captain of the guard of Nottingham Castle. I can identify most of the others by name, but for the moment I'll just ensure that they step down onto the grass, ready to be apprehended. I hope they'll be walking all the way to London.'

'They will be unless we can commandeer some wagons locally,' Brindley said.

Just then, the man known to Constable Giles as Jem Bolger grabbed Francis from behind and pulled him backwards by his hair, then produced a long knife. He drew it across Francis's throat in a threatening gesture and said, 'I go free, else this precious bailiff gets his throat slit.'

It fell silent, although the look of fear in Francis's eyes spoke loudly enough. Edward was assessing his distance away from Francis and trying to decide the best way to come to his rescue when Robbie Bishop loomed up behind Bolger and gripped his throat.

'Drop the knife, else I'll squeeze your poxy throat like a ripe orange,' he hissed, and the knife seemed to drop lifelessly from Bolger's hand as his eyes bulged and saliva began to dribble from his mouth. He was only able to utter one grating sound before Robbie relinquished his grip and kneed Bolger in the small of his back with enough force to send him sprawling forward onto the grass, where a uniformed member of the Tower guard was ordered to retrieve him and tie his hands behind his back.

The same fate befell all those who Edward was able to identify as their former captors. Meanwhile, Francis rode back into Skegby to acquire several wagons, into which those arrested on charges of treason were loaded prior to the entire contingent starting on the road south, following grateful thanks from Edward and Francis. Rose left the cover of the trees in front of the farmhouse in order to treat the slight cut to Francis's neck that he'd sustained from Bolger's knife.

Francis discharged his constables with many thanks for their loyal service, and apologies for their enforced incarceration inside the Whitely farmhouse. He then told them that they might regard the forthcoming week as an additional holiday from their duties. Edward told his constables that he couldn't be quite as generous, but that he wouldn't expect to see any of them in the muster room of the Guildhall until the following Monday, which was four days away, given that it was now Thursday. Robbie was about to leave with them when Francis called him back.

'Where do you think *you're* going?' he asked with mock severity.

Robbie's gaze fell to the grass at his feet. 'I was thinking of going home to my wife and kids, sir,' he replied, then looked uncertainly in Edward's direction for confirmation that this would be allowed. Before he could reply, Francis beat him to it.

'You're going nowhere until you've eaten a hearty meal at a certain apple orchard in Daybrook,' he said. 'And Bailiff Mountsorrel's invited as well.'

After the joyful homecoming, tearful embraces, and far too much cider, Edward and Robbie sat around the table in the Daybrook house with Francis's family for a massive late supper, over which they exchanged stories.

'I take it that Rose was simply creating a distraction while Robbie slipped into the farmhouse the back way?'

'That's right,' Rose said. 'I was able to sneak into the trees while the rest of you were being taken into the house. Then I wandered back as far as the constable's house in Hucknall, wondering what to do next. His lovely wife Mary insisted that I stay for as long as it took for help to arrive, and of course I learned from her that there were soldiers coming up from London. What I hadn't expected was to see Robbie guiding them on their way, and when we caught up again we devised that ploy to get him into the back of the house.'

'Where he saved my life,' Edward told Rose and Kitty, 'showing extreme bravery by stepping in front of a man armed with a loaded crossbow. That makes him a hero in my book, although I imagine that Francis will continue to insult him in future.'

'How could I do that, when he saved my life as well, grabbing that man who had a knife at my throat?'

'I told you he was a lovely man, didn't I?' Rose chuckled. 'I hope that he'll be suitably rewarded in due course.'

'I don't imagine that there'll be any reward,' Edward told them, 'but I'll certainly be putting in a *very* complimentary report regarding his bravery and accomplishments.'

'I'll just be happy to go home, sir,' Robbie muttered, red in the face with embarrassment. 'And I did what I did without thinking afore doing it.'

'They say that true heroes are men without imagination,' Edward assured him, 'and that probably includes Francis now.'

'Meaning what, precisely?' Francis challenged.

'Your actions with that crossbow. I don't believe that you've ever had occasion to use one, have you?'

'No, as it happens,' Francis confirmed. 'But was it that obvious?'

'Only to me, probably, but it's as well that you weren't called upon to fire it,' said Edward with great amusement. 'You had the bolt in back to front.'

17

'Why did he tell us to come alone?' Francis asked as he and Edward turned off the road that led to Ashby village and began the final leg of their journey, up the long drive that led to the castle, where they'd been summoned to take dinner with the Earl of Huntingdon.

'No idea,' Edward replied, pulling on Oliver's reins as saw the cottage approaching, 'but Elizabeth insisted that I call in and see how her father's managing with being a widower. Although not, I suspect, a lonely one.'

He was proved right when he and Francis pushed open the cottage door and saw Edwin Porter and Madge Catchpole move guiltily apart from where they appeared to have been holding hands. Edward pretended not to notice as he called out breezily, 'We can't stop for food and drink or anything, since we're invited to take dinner in the big house. I can see that you've had yours,' he added as he nodded towards the leftover pie on the table. 'I just need to reassure Elizabeth that you're in good health, and of not too mournful a disposition. Can I report that you are doing well?'

'What do *you* think?' Edwin replied grumpily. 'Just tell her that I want for nothing — and give me warning of your intended arrival next time.'

'Do you think they were — you know?' Francis asked after they'd remounted, and had the crenulated ramparts of the castle in sight.

Edward chuckled. 'So what if they were? Good for them, I say. Anyway, here we are, and it looks as if we're expected.'

They dismounted and handed their horses' reins to Pip, the fresh-faced young groom who walked out of the stables to meet them with a friendly wave. He remembered the generous gift he'd received from Edward on a previous occasion.

They walked towards the front door, where the steward was awaiting them. 'Now let's see what we have to do to earn our dinner,' said Edward.

The earl rose to meet them inside the grand hall, where the board had already been set, and a familiar fellow guest was already in attendance, and gazing down eagerly at the various roast dishes.

'You will, I assume, remember Walter Emerson?' the earl asked. 'I should perhaps tell you that he's now *Sir* Walter Emerson, thanks to your recent success in bringing in those traitors, along with others like yourselves who performed similar services for the Crown around the nation.'

'And we are presumably summoned here to learn the outcome of all those investigations?' Edward guessed.

Emerson nodded. 'You are indeed, but I am anxious to partake of this excellent repast, so shall we lose no more time about it? And will you leave any questions until I have finished?'

Edward and Francis agreed, and Emerson cast his eyes up at the ornately carved ceiling as he began.

'You will probably have concluded for yourselves that Calvert was the main instigator of what was planned for Nottingham Castle. Indeed, his was the evil hand behind all the proposed uprisings outside London, timed to occur immediately after the successful explosion inside the Palace of Westminster. When it failed to occur, Calvert nevertheless decided to persevere with his part in the overall plot, and he opted to do so from the comparative safety of Nottingham, where he could rely on support from his old friend Aaron Drucker. What Calvert failed to realise was that all the remaining main conspirators at the London end of the matter had either been captured or were in hiding. Even had Calvert succeeded, his efforts would have achieved little more than either the destruction of a fine old fortress, or its threatened destruction as some sort of bargaining piece for the release of men like Fawkes and Catesby.'

'I'm not sure he was that loyal to those he'd become involved with,' Edward observed.

'You are probably wondering what persuaded Captain Makepeace to throw in his hand with the conspirators. The answer to that may be found in his own personal ambitions, and his belief that his services had not been adequately rewarded by those currently in power. That, and the fact that he owed Drucker a considerable sum of money by virtue of gambling debts that Drucker had covered for him, seemingly out of generosity, but in reality in order to have control over a man who could be central to any plot involving the castle that he was employed to guard. It would seem that the gunpowder was never intended to be lit — merely stored in the passageways in the rock beneath the castle, with the threat that it could be set off at any time if the rebels' demands were not met.'

'Whitely?' Francis enquired.

'I was coming to him,' Emerson responded curtly. 'Calvert obviously needed two things when he first arrived in the area, and was hidden away by a relative of the main conspirator Robert Keyes, who was already in custody. As you probably know, that man was Jamie Saunders, who was a stepson of Keyes's brother Ralph. Through the Keyes connection, Saunders knew of a man in Nottingham who also had a brother confined for his Catholic beliefs — Thomas Whitely, who had a double attraction for Calvert. First of all, Whitely had a house in the town that could be conveniently used to hide the barrels of gunpowder that Drucker had already begun to import through the ill-managed port facility at Sutton Bridge, prior to its being loaded into the castle under the cover of darkness, aided, of course, by Captain Makepeace. But Calvert could hardly believe his good fortune when he learned that this same Thomas Whitely was the proprietor of an alehouse cut into the rock on which the castle stood, and from which it could be accessed by way of a series of tunnels.'

He paused for breath, but his eyes warned his audience not to interrupt as he completed the picture.

'We shall probably never know what exactly transpired, but it would seem that despite going along with the plan initially, in the belief that he would be helping to free his brother from captivity, Whitely seemed to change his mind at the last moment, refusing to hand over his alehouse keys to Calvert. From what you were able to discover, Mountsorrel, it appears to have been the case that Calvert acquired the keys anyway by bribing a servant in the Whitely house, and was then confronted by Whitely with a demand for their return. In the ensuing argument, it would seem that a pistol was carelessly discharged, leading to the explosion and fire that first drew the authorities to the house in Halifax Lane. And there, I think, you have the complete picture.'

'Not quite,' Edward ventured, as Emerson began cutting himself a generous slice from the venison haunch that had been tempting him for the best part of an hour. 'What has happened to all those you mention, and what of the minor players — the ones from Skegby and its surrounds?'

'Drucker and Makepeace will be hung, drawn and quartered, without the need for any great legal formality, given their enthusiasm to make admissions under the ministrations of those employed in the Tower to acquire them. Saunders, Wilbert and the like — some ten in number — will take their chances at trial, with a special plea for clemency on behalf of Wilbert, should he be found guilty, to reflect his willingness to peach on the others. As for Sheriff Gamble, the charges against him have been reduced, at the specific intervention of the attorney general who regrets having appointed him. He will simply be accused of evading the tunnage tax. Even so, he will be disgraced, and his estates will be forfeit. Anything further, or may I begin to enjoy my dinner?'

For the next hour, they all savoured the most succulent of meats, the juiciest of fruits, the tartest of cheeses and the sweetest of fruit flans, all washed down with a fine choice of claret and sauterne. They avoided conversing about affairs of State, confining themselves to mundane topics such as the weather, the decline in moral standards among the young, and the likely harvest from the upcoming summer. It was during this segment of the conversation that the earl expressed his frustration with a problem besetting his estate.

'As you had occasion to note, we enjoy the finest venison from our upper pasture. However, of late we have been troubled by the attentions of those who also wish to sample the quality of our estate-reared beasts, but without payment. In the main we believe them to be from the local village, or perhaps one of the settlements further south, closer to Leicester, but not even when we raised the fence heights did their depredations show any sign of lessening.'

'I worked on a large landed estate before becoming a soldier,' Edward told the earl and his other guest, 'and my experience was that the only successful way of avoiding poachers was to guarantee that they would get caught, and receive either a trip to the local magistrate or an arrow up the … well, a well-placed shaft, anyway.'

'So you are a soldier with experience of estate management?' the earl observed. 'That must surely be an unusual combination of talents.'

'Only one of which made me fit to be a bailiff,' Edward observed sadly. 'I value those times when I can bring my family here on a visit to my father-in-law, who served as your father's steward, since then I can once again breathe in the honest fragrance of the woodland, and enjoy the assorted evening birdsong as a prelude to sleep.'

'Give me the bustle and energy of the town any day,' Emerson replied as he washed his fingers for the final time in the lemon-infused water bowl, wiped them on his napkin, and sat back with a contented sigh. 'All I seem to do when I visit rural locations is sneeze. And as for those revolting animal smells — well, enough said, I think.'

'But you must tire of constantly having to guard your purse from thieving hands?' Francis pointed out.

Emerson shook his head. 'There are *some* privileges to being directly in the service of the Crown, and a heavily armed escort is one of them. No doubt those who rode alongside the coach that brought me here are even now being richly rewarded by the earl's excellent cook. And the mention of rewards reminds me that I had, in my eagerness to dine, forgotten something else that I have to tell you both.'

It fell silent, and all eyes — including the earl's — were on Emerson as he announced, 'In recognition of your highly valued service to His Majesty, he has instructed the Chancellor to bestow some sort of financial reward upon you.

Unfortunately, Thomas Egerton is one of the more parsimonious of those who have ever occupied that office, but nevertheless I would imagine that an annual pension to each of you of seventy pounds, for the remainder of your lives, will be more gratefully received than a poke in the eye?'

Edward and Francis were still finding ways of expressing their astonished thanks when Emerson rose to leave, and was escorted to the door by his host. Edward and Francis took the hint and rose from the table, heading for the same door, until the earl pulled Edward back by the sleeve of his doublet. 'A moment of your time, if you would, Master Mountsorrel.'

Francis waited patiently outside the stables with the two saddled horses until Edward rejoined him only minutes later. 'What was all that about?' he demanded.

'Later,' Edward said. 'Next Friday coming, in fact, when you, Kitty, Rose and your children are invited to dine with us. I have chosen Friday because that is the day when the fishmonger is most plentifully supplied, and experience has shown that Margaret, who insists on doing the cooking, is less poisonous in her efforts with fish than with other items. She is of course supervised by Meg, but has this tendency to over-spice things when Meg has her back turned. You will be welcome nevertheless.'

'I'm not sure, at this moment, that I can even contemplate more food,' Francis groaned, 'but I accept, even if, as usual, you make me burn with curiosity.'

When Friday came around, Edward and his family grew a little concerned when the nearby church of St Nicholas chimed out noon, and there was still no sign of their guests. But just as Meg was suggesting that she place the baked perch on a metal tray above the griddle in order to keep it warm, there was a hammering on the front door, and in walked Francis without further invitation, Kitty and Rose in his wake. Robert raced outside to engage Richard and Amy in some mischief, and Joanna followed him out. Elizabeth held on to young Edwin and firmly instructed him to sit back down on his chair.

'My apologies for our tardiness,' Francis said breezily, 'but I took the opportunity to call in on Robbie Bishop, and now I have a confession to make.'

'What on earth are you drivelling on about?' Edward asked.

'I just lost you one of your finest constables — the young man with whom we have been working so closely,' Francis admitted.

'I never expected to hear you say that about poor old Robbie,' said Edward, 'so why the change of heart? And why did you take it upon yourself to dismiss one of my men?'

'He saved my life — and yours, for that matter — so the reason for my amended opinion is, I would have thought, obvious. But the second part of my news is that Robbie is being transferred to the county, in a promoted office.' Francis paused as Edward stared at him. 'As you will be aware, Sheriff Sutton's term of office came to an end today. As his final act, I persuaded him that there was a need for a constable out at Skegby, and that given the level of lawlessness out there, and the proximity of the county border, the position should be designated as one befitting a senior constable. I was more than happy to recommend Robbie for it. The harder part was persuading Robbie himself, until I mentioned that the fine old former farmhouse that once belonged to the Whitely family, then fell to the Saunders brood who are shortly to forfeit it to the Crown for their crimes, would be an ideal place to bring up six children. Robbie remembered it well, and since it is the place where he saved both our lives, it seemed appropriate.'

'So Robbie gets a reward as well,' Edward mused as he waved the guests to the table, and asked Margaret to set about serving the wine. 'And of course you'll have a trusted man to do your bidding out on your western border.'

It fell uncomfortably silent as Kitty and Rose looked down at the table, leaving Francis to cough nervously and reply, 'Not me, Edward. My successor, whoever that will be.'

'You're handing in your club, sword and badge of office?' Edward asked with amusement.

'Indeed I am,' Francis confirmed. 'Seventy pounds a year guaranteed was all the incentive I needed to finally try my hand, full time, at being an apple farmer. Kitty and Rose are *very* supportive of the suggestion, and…'

'And in fact we *insisted*,' Rose said. 'It wasn't even Francis's idea in the first place.'

Kitty nodded with a smile that was almost coquettish, then said, 'My only regret is that I'll be depriving you of a valued and trusted colleague.'

'You won't,' Edward replied, then hastened to correct the impression that he might have just created. 'Not to say that Francis wasn't a valued and trusted colleague. Just that he wouldn't have been mine any longer anyway.'

'Francis isn't the only one who can talk in riddles,' Elizabeth chimed in. 'What my husband means is that from the first day of next month, he'll be employed as the grounds master of Ashby Castle and we'll all be living in that dower house in which Edwin and Amy were born.'

'That was what you kept from me as we were leaving Ashby?' Francis asked. 'The old fossil made you an offer?'

'A very generous one,' Edward confirmed. 'Now, unless anyone else has a dark secret that they need to get off their conscience, I suggest that we eat. Rose can deal with any malady that ensues afterwards.'

Two hours later, as their guests were taking their leave, Francis was almost in tears as he turned to shake Edward's hand. 'I suppose that this is the last time,' he choked.

Edward raised his eyebrows as he asked, 'Does that mean that we're no longer welcome at Daybrook?'

'No, far from it, as I hope that we will be welcome visitors at Ashby. It's just that, well — you know how it is — the best of friendships have been known to dissolve during extended absence.'

'Look across the road,' Edward instructed him with a nod towards the house directly opposite his. Its predecessor had been maliciously burned down many years ago in an attempt to kill both men when they had shared the dwelling as part of their duties. It was there that their friendship had developed and deepened, and now the house was occupied by the town's clerk of markets. 'I often stand here of an evening and recall those times when we lived together, before I met Elizabeth, and in the days when you were pursuing plump widows. We formed a friendship then that has survived almost every kind of obstacle you could imagine, including your stupidity at times.'

'Not to mention your impetuosity,' Francis retorted as he grasped Edward's hand, then flung his arms around him. 'Farewell, Bailiff Mountsorrel,' he mumbled.

'And goodbye, Bailiff Barton,' Edward replied as he fought back tears of his own. Then he added one final thought. 'Someone else can keep the peace in our absence. And I wish them the best of luck.'

A NOTE TO THE READER

Dear Reader,

Thank you for taking the time to read this sixth and final novel in the Bailiff Mountsorrel Tudor Mystery series; I hope you approve of the career changes that I awarded Edward and Francis. One of the great attractions of writing this series has been the opportunity to research the early history of Nottingham, where I was born and raised, although Edward and Francis would not recognise it today.

There is nothing left of the town as it would have been in their day, apart from a few street names that recall the occupations and trades of those who lived in them. Those mentioned in the series that still exist in name only include Bridlesmith Gate (for many years now a 'pedestrian only' thoroughfare), Barker Gate ('barker' being an early name for a tanner), and Fletcher Gate, named after the 'fleshers', or butchers, who established their businesses there. Halifax Lane, where the explosion and fire launched Edward's enquiries in this novel, is now known as Halifax Place, and it was originally named, not after the town in Yorkshire, but an early mayor of the town, William Halifax.

In the novel, the Guildhall is the seat of civic government in the town, and the immediate area of Weekday Cross boasts a daily market. This all disappeared in the 1970s due to an act of architectural vandalism that resulted in the creation of the Broadmarsh Centre, a commercial shopping complex that bankrupted itself fifty years later, and at the time of writing is now a massive hole in the ground.

At least the castle remains, although hardly in the form it took in the early seventeenth century. The old medieval structure that came under threat of demolition by gunpowder in this novel was in fact destroyed on the orders of its own governor at the end of the Civil War, to be replaced by a Georgian eyesore that was little more than an upper-class boarding house until taken over by the city council in the late Victorian era. A recent attempt to commercialise it left it looking like a medieval Disneyland, but that too failed financially. Officially the cause of that failure was the COVID lockdown, but I prefer to believe that public taste prevailed.

However, the civic fathers could do little to ruin the rock on which the castle still stands — over one hundred and thirty feet of soft sandstone into which generations of residents cut caves and linked passageways. The series of tunnels that lead down from the building above, winding their way down to ground level, have served as dwellings, dungeons, storage places and eerie locations for tours in which ghost stories are recounted to eager tourists by skilled guides. And once they come out at street level, they do so in a public house — the same one that is described in this and previous novels, but which today fulfils a different role.

Ask any student from one of modern Nottingham's two universities where they like to drink, and they are likely to reply 'Ye Olde Trip to Jerusalem'. Tradition has it that this was once the meeting place for those intending to embark on a crusade, given that the word 'tryppe' is an old English word for 'halt'. Whether or not this ancient establishment with a few resident ghosts dates back to this time, there was certainly an alehouse on the site in Edward Mountsorrel's day, and it was indeed called The Pilgrim. Prior to that, as indicated in the pages you have just read, the building served as a brewery for the castle, and the name 'Brewhouse Yard' has lived on as the location of a row of buildings that once housed lace workers who made use of the water they drew from the River Leen, which ran past their front doors. Today the row is home to the 'Museum of Nottingham Life'.

As for the River Leen itself, it's still there, but some yards away from its original course, and culverted. Which is perhaps as well, given that it had become a substantial health hazard following the Industrial Revolution.

Those unfamiliar with the history of weaponry may have been surprised by the reference in this novel to the use of firearms. They had in fact begun to feature in warfare by this time, but the type that was described as having caused the explosion in the house on Halifax Lane — the 'firelock' — was one of the earliest and crudest, posing as much danger to the user as the intended victim. It required the manual application of a lighted fuse to the touch hole, which in turn set off the flash pan that fired the shot — a ball of lead that had been first loaded down the barrel. It would over time evolve into the rapid fire assault rifles with which modern soldiers are equipped.

The general plot of the novel was the result of research beyond the bare bones of the Gunpowder Plot that we all learned about at school, with Guy Fawkes as the alleged leader of the failed coup. In fact he was merely the man delegated the job of lighting the fuse, who got caught twelve hours before the appointed time. (You might say of him that 'He had one job…'). The true leaders of the intended rebellion were men like Robert Catesby, Thomas Percy and Robert Keyes — the same Robert Keyes who features in this novel. The slaughter of those gathered for the State Opening of Parliament on 5th November was intended as the prelude to the establishment of a new order, with the little Princess Elizabeth as the titular monarch, but the real power being handed back to Rome. When the first stage of the plot failed, those responsible fled to the various 'safe' country houses that they'd established. It then became apparent that a whole network existed beneath those who were being tortured in the Tower, and it fell to local law enforcement professionals to identify them and flush them out into the open.

The term 'bailiff' lives on, and is probably more familiar to you as the person from whom debtors hide when they arrive to take possession of their property. In many common law jurisdictions they are also responsible for the security and management of a jury during the course of a criminal trial. Their diminishing role as law enforcement officers coincided with the establishment of local police forces and the reorganisation of the criminal justice process, but for the middle years in English history there would have been many Mountsorrels and Bartons keeping the peace and bringing offenders to justice.

As this series comes to an end, I genuinely hope that these novels provided a few hours of pleasant diversion and a convincing step back in time.

As ever, I would be delighted to see a review of my book posted on **Amazon** or **Goodreads**. Alternatively, feel free to visit, and contact me on, my author website: **davidfieldauthor.com**.

Happy reading!
David

Sapere Books is an exciting new publisher of brilliant fiction and popular history.

To find out more about our latest releases and our monthly bargain books visit our website: **saperebooks.com**

Printed in Dunstable, United Kingdom